# FAILED SUMMER VACATION

# FAILED SUMMER VACATION

Heuijung Hur

Translated by
Paige Aniyah Morris

# Contents

# FAILED SUMMER
# VACATION

# Flying in the Rain

There were always spare flowerpots in the greenhouse.

It had taken a while to realise the building was called a greenhouse, taken just as long to learn that the things crammed inside the greenhouse were called flowerpots and that their whole purpose was to serve as receptacles for growing plants. *Greenhouse. Flowerpot.* Such strange words – not many people left who knew them.

Why do people grow plants anyway?

Well, all sorts of reasons. You can use them for food, plus they're nice to look at. Though maybe the most important reason is because they produce oxygen.

You mean $O_2$?

Yeah. People breathed oxygen back then.

Q explains this as he trims the overgrown shoots from a plant. The thick glass walls of the greenhouse block out all the noise from outside, and the artificial lights overhead are so bright it's impossible to look at them straight on. The protective gloves Q is wearing are thick and encumber his hands. He's accidentally clipping the gloves with his scissors, but the metal-ceramic casing is so sturdy that the rusted blades don't leave a mark. All the time, G stares in wonder at Q's unscathed hands. Snipped-off stems fall to the ground, green on endless green. Q lets go of the plant he had been holding. It sways from side to side before settling into place. Its leaves rustle, the lights catching on the fine hairs that lie along their edges.

G watches for a moment before he turns to go. Water rolls down the glass face of the greenhouse in little beads. The rain today is a quiet, steady rain – not like the downpour that fell the previous night. G walks away, leaving the greenhouse behind.

*

These were the sorts of scenes G remembered when he closed his eyes, memories like a well-designed algorithm. When he input the action (closing his eyes), the program would generate certain scenes on an endless loop. The more of them he watched, unable to pause or intervene, the lower his chances were of being able to fall asleep.

Passengers were advised to sleep while travelling through space. Though this measure was no longer mandatory as it had been a century ago, many travellers still did. On return flights to the Union especially, most passengers made the trip back in a state of sleep, the whole spaceship submerged in silence. It was the simplest way to escape the unpleasant thoughts that wormed their way into the limited space and unlimited time on the ship, which was why G also opted to sleep. Even though his attempts so far had been unsuccessful.

G was one of the few survivors of that final expedition, and a key witness in the case of Q's disappearance. All the survivors were required to undergo counselling. Prior to this the counsellor had existed for them as only a name, and he never seemed to know what to ask or what he was even driving at with his questions. It was appalling.

When not in the counselling sessions, G tried to pass the time in his sleep capsule. But it was no use. Thanks to the unerring algorithm, any time he closed his eyes he was overrun with memories of Q. Like an orchard blooming without anyone tending it.

\*

Q took meticulous care of the plants. The only living things in that region of Earth were the crew members and a mass of impossibly overgrown plants – and it was probably only the chloroplasts he felt any affection for. Most of that long, chaotic expedition, Q spent in the greenhouse. He watered the plants, checked the condition of the soil, provided them with adequate organic matter, observed and recorded the shapes of the leaves and the appearance of the stems. And, as if to repay him for his devotion, you could see the greenhouse plants growing by the day.

Although the same went for the plants outside too, maybe even more than those indoors. But of course that was only natural. After all, the plants in the greenhouse had come from the wild. Ever since he first started cultivating the plants, we had wanted to know: what was his aim? What was he trying to do?

G swallowed and then, just as he opened his mouth to say more, the bell sounded. His session was over. G pursed his lips, stood up, and pushed in his chair. The next person would be coming in soon. He thought back to the conversation he'd had with Q about what he was doing. He remembered how Q had feigned ignorance then, like he hadn't understood what G was asking.

G didn't like plants. He thought they were a menace, a grotesque alien life form. Trees and grasses grew everywhere with abandon, shooting up unfettered in dense, leafy clusters, invading territory keenly. These were the simple conditions of their survival. But G was terrified of that simplicity which made it so much harder for him to understand Q's attachment to the greenhouse. Although he did take a strange kind of pleasure in watching the process of plant domestication. G never admitted it to anyone, but there were times he went with Q on his visits to the greenhouse not just because they had to travel in twos but because he got to watch Q with the plants.

One of the most basic rules of the expedition was that all activities on Earth had to be conducted in pairs. To prevent anyone from getting stranded. You had to keep a close eye on your partner at all times, and if you noticed anything even the slightest bit suspicious, you had to report it. It was meant to protect the crew members as they explored, the landscape altered in unknown ways after the catastrophe. If someone was abandoned there, they would die a painful death, starving and suffocating in the unbreathable atmosphere. It wouldn't be long before their body became yet another vessel through which the invasive life forms would spread.

G was careful to avoid dying like this. He wanted to live, to become a successful engineer, to have the financially stable life that came with the position, to grow old and happy with people he loved. As soon as he graduated from the institute, he found a job at the Interplanetary Union's research centre. He thought it the best career decision he could have made.

The research centre studied the survival and adaptation of Union constituents throughout space. After the disaster, humans had been forced to live scattered across a multitude of wildly different planets, although none of them had been able to adapt to any one planet without issue. Which was why the research centre was set up: to ensure the continued survival of humankind.

Of course there had been private institutions with a similar mission before. But none of them compared to the research centre, which possessed massive amounts of data and advanced technologies, as well as the government backing that came with Interplanetary Union affiliation. The planets in the Union spared no expense when it came to investments and support. Working for the research centre would give G a great opportunity to achieve his ambitions as an engineer and work alongside the greatest scientists of his generation. A privilege he only began to question when he was assigned to the Return to Earth project.

*

*In vivo experimentation.*

Words that no one in the conference room dared to say. But, remembering them now, G felt goosebumps prickling his skin. Like *greenhouse* and *flowerpot*, *in vivo experimentation* was a phrase he had not heard for a long time. Living things, including humans, hadn't been used in experiments since the previous century. But what Q had suggested seemed no different from an in vivo experiment, one with live human subjects. Only an extremist Returnee could have put forward such an idea.

G objected to this completely, and the rest of the crew felt the same way. Yes, they were having trouble with their equipment and communications with the research centre, but G was adamant the situation did not warrant such an extreme response. As soon as he voiced his concerns, though, he was met with opposition from Q. The situation may not be that bad now, he said. But we can't rely only on our existing resources when we don't know how or even when things will be resolved.

No one else spoke, and G couldn't tell if Q was beginning to persuade them.

G returned to his quarters and took off his helmet. The air felt familiar. Breathing came intuitively. He had the sudden urge to move around the base like this. But as an employee of the Union Research Centre, he was required to wear his respirator at all times, a rule intended to create a sense of parity despite everyone's different capacities to breathe on Earth. Yet G felt a sense of discord had already spread enough to saturate the atmosphere inside that conference room.

Until communications with the Union were restored and the crew able to notify them that a part of the research vessel had been destroyed, Q believed they could prolong their survival by actively cultivating, harvesting, and consuming plants. And increasingly, G was surprised to find people had begun to agree with Q. Wasn't this, they insisted, an inevitable step if their aim was indeed to return to Earth? This, they explained, would be the rational conclusion. But G couldn't agree with them. He thought them deluded and naive and possibly also a bit stupid.

Most of the people who initially agreed with Q came from similar regions as him, the descendants of those who'd just about managed to adapt to life on a barren planet. Infant survival rate amongst these people had been low, their life expectancy shorter than on other planets in the Union and even the regions where people suffered the syndromes and complications that came from adapting to space. These people couldn't help but hold onto a certain fantasy about Earth. But G considered the return they dreamed of as absurd and backward, the very idea of a homecoming seeming to contradict their position as members of the Union. G lay in bed, staring at the ceiling, the old prejudices he had tried to contain seeping out with every breath.

*

G knew the Returnees' argument: the conditions of each planet varied tremendously; even after several centuries, humans still hadn't been able to adapt perfectly to any of them. The problems posed by each environment were specific, individual, and existential. The only way to resolve these problems, Returnees said, was to return to Earth.

Which made no sense to G. The Union Research Centre had been established to solve the problems humans were facing. Of course, the centre could not tackle every problem on every planet; there would always be some more urgent than others but, all things considered, the number of issues the research centre had resolved was impressive. The Returnees did not give the centre enough credit, not acknowledging how naturally they'd been able to breathe here.

It wasn't an issue of having the technology for a return to Earth. What they lacked was sufficient time and the intel. The research centre knew astonishingly little about how Earth's environment had changed after those who'd been able to leave had abandoned the planet, and their researchers were still working through scores of unresolved issues on other planets. All in all, there had never been much opportunity to find out more about Earth and the changes it had undergone. Which led people to doubt the veracity of Returnees' views.

There was some literature about Earth. But most of it focused on life before the disaster. The old stories had been taken apart and re-assembled so many times over the generations that they had turned Earth into some folkloric homeland, alien and majestic, omitting from their accounts the cowards who had abandoned the homeland and those left behind.

The sudden interest in the idea of a return came from the Interplanetary Union's election of a new leader, who announced that during his tenure he would initiate plans for the first expedition in a forthcoming Return project.

Scientists drafted hypotheses, ran simulations and presented papers, although their claims were all based on out-of-date information. For, while unmanned probes began making regular trips to and from Earth, they never touched down on the surface. All sorts of reasons were given for this – the drastic shifts Earth's surface had undergone, the damage it might do to the machines, the likely cost of recovery missions. But the general feeling underlying each of the reasons was the same: fear – that what they imagined might be nothing like the reality, that every belief they had held onto all this time might be shattered.

*

The flight was long. Travelling between planets, the ship flew with relative ease and stability but the moment it entered Earth's atmosphere all of that suddenly changed.

They crossed from the thermosphere into the stratosphere without any issues, though it was on descending into the troposphere that the alarm began to sound.

Droplets of some unknown liquid were beating down on the ship's exterior; no one could tell their weight or density or composition, or even the damage they might cause to the vessel. All they knew was that they were impacting the spacecraft's flight in strange ways. And, worse, the Earth's atmosphere itself seemed to be unstable. They urgently recalibrated their approach to the landing site, eventually touching down a distance away.

It was technically a crash landing, and they were lucky their ship wasn't destroyed in the process. Checking for damage, they found the ship secure and still operational. But the expedition team couldn't bring themselves to disembark right away. The idea of unknown terrain and a mission with no precedent sent emotions of all colours and textures coursing through them. Soon, they would be taking the first steps on the very earth that no other human of their generation had seen.

\*

I remember the hatch door opening. As the unit touched the ground, our internal displays lit up green. I'm not exaggerating when I tell you everything we saw was covered in it. Not only the land, but the remains of what were clearly human-made structures. I'd never seen anything like it.

Honestly, I thought the crash landing had affected my display until I heard the crew in the other units complaining of the same thing, all of us adjusting our screens' brightness, to no avail: all we could see was the greenery.

Once my eyes had adjusted to the surroundings, I realised the clusters formed different shapes. Some were long and outstretched, and others were wide and flat, some small and spongy, others vast and sprawling, all of them different shades. It was uncanny. You've probably seen something like this in photos. It was – how can I put it? Overwhelming.

The speakers crackled then, and I heard the voice of the operator on the main ship.

They're plants.

A lot of noise was cutting in, but I heard him through the screech of feedback. The sound went right through me, and I felt a terrible chill in my bones.

Looking more closely, I saw the plants swaying a little, the smaller offshoots and their even thinner sprouts trembling slightly. I remembered then the falling droplets were a compound of oxygen, hydrogen and trace minerals. They made an incessant rustling sound like white noise. Yes, exactly – it was raining.

*

I suppose that first expedition was something of a success. We found the Earth's environment more hospitable than we had expected. The greatest evidence of this was that plants were growing again across the entire planet. In the long time that had passed, no one could rule out the possibility that the plants had mutated to become something unknown, but everyone was hopeful the Earth's ecosystem showed signs of being restored.

It was the weather that proved the issue. For the duration of the trip, approximately ninety Earth days, there wasn't a single day without rain. Long days of thin, misty drizzle that settled quietly; days where it came down in torrents, in sheets. Some days a heavy downpour would start and subside just as suddenly, while other days blustering winds blew the rain about endlessly.

The surface of the Earth was forever sopping wet, and every step of ours took us further and further into moist, squishy mud. The boggy ground was covered in decomposing matter, on top of which sat slightly less rotted matter, on top of which sat matter that was yet to start rotting. Any movement spattered mud and congealed clumps of wet leaves at you. The rush of rain and leaves obscured our sight; flecks of mud dried and got caked into the narrow crevices of the safety equipment, causing minor malfunctions. It grew more and more important that we adapted our equipment and our plans to account for the weather.

The first expedition crew drafted a report of their main findings. They felt sure it would prove a tremendous help to future expeditions. It seemed there really would come a day when humans might be able to return to Earth.

No one on the crew could have imagined the report would be returned to them, rejected. The Interplanetary Union's response was terse and, for reasons he wouldn't explain, the captain refused to tell his expedition team what he knew. The issue could have been anything – maybe, the crew thought, there was growing public opposition to the idea of a return mission. Either way, the expedition team couldn't accept the Union's directive to amend the contents of the report. They asked for more information, but the captain's response was the same: communications with the Union, he said, were not simple.

As a result, dissent began to grow, from those who wanted the whole mission aborted to those who simply wished for better conditions. But discussion made no difference; none of them had any choice, and so they spent the remainder of the expedition revising the report. Rewriting conclusive sentences to be less conclusive, explicit references to be less explicit, weighing down assertive sentences with possibilities.

However, instead of working on the report, G often found his partner zoning out, looking utterly drained.

*

At first, I thought he was just one of the usual Returnees. One of those people who lived their lives clinging to those ridiculous fantasies. What other reason could there be? I saw that where everyone else on the expedition seemed simply deflated by the rejected report, he took it especially hard. At mealtimes, when the crew would discuss the project and its future, he never once joined in the conversation, finishing his meal and heading back to his quarters without saying a word. I agree – he seemed depressed. But even then, I never thought of him as dangerous.

It was him who needed the counselling, not me. But as I'm sure you know, the return project ran into a lot of trouble, not only financial but also administrative: there seemed to be no central organisation behind it at all. Which meant – you're right – we were never assigned counsellors. For a long time, there was nothing but a nameplate on the desk you're sitting at right now. I know – it was a violation of the rules. But back then, we bent more rules than I can name. There was no one to file a complaint to. Maybe if there had been, I would have said something. Yes, I was his partner. But I was anxious as well. Just like everyone else on the team. Right – right. I think what I'm trying to say is there was nothing I could have done.

In all honesty, I didn't think he was a good fit for the expedition. Sure, behind a desk, stubbornness may be a useful skill. I'm sure it's helped loads of scientists tackle complex problems. But, as you know, many of the last century's problems have been solved by now. All that matters now are the tasks we're still to face. Improving child mortality rates, designing a respirator that can be used on all planets across the Union; settling the culture wars between the pro- and anti-Union factions, overcoming the difficulties migrants face adapting to their planets – those sorts of things.

Q tended to approach every problem from an extreme point of view, which is why we always argued. But I want to make it 100% clear that any fights we had were down to nothing more than differences of opinion.

Either way, I'm sure others saw that we didn't get on. We hardly ever talked about anything personal, and when it came to work, our opinions were so opposed that I often ended up raising my voice at him – yelling. But I don't think you can say I did something to harm him just because of how things *appeared*.

*

It took a while before the expedition could continue. The problem was the oxygen. The plants that had overtaken the Earth's surface were emitting it endlessly. Which meant the composition of the Earth's atmosphere was not only much altered from centuries before, but also nothing like the air they had become used to on other planets. Those who lived in space, for example, had evolved to no longer breathe oxygen.

The issues fed everyone's misgivings about a manned expedition in that sort of environment. Their arguments grew more shrill. The Union government and the research centre held long negotiations. There were loud and very public denunciations, but because the report had not been released to the public, it wasn't clear who opposed what. G imagined the project would be called off soon. Or – more accurately – he hoped it would be. No matter what they discovered on Earth, the findings would only be dismissed. It felt so inevitable G refused to let it bother him.

In the end, they resumed the mission with a drastically reduced budget and remit. The crew on the ground were mostly just entry-level researchers – G and Q among them. And just like all the other research centre projects, they had to sign a contract accepting all the risks that came with the expedition, although the language in the waiver seemed different to how they had read it before.

The landing on a new site was no simpler than it had been the first time. The crew were almost familiar with the incessant wail of the collision alarms the moment they entered the planet's atmosphere, until the moment they touched down on the surface. Unable to make out their colleagues' voices above all the other noise, they weren't able to change the coordinates of their predetermined route, and so had to resign themselves to the fact that they were essentially landing blind. And though it was officially their duty to respond to new situations, none of them did anything as they descended.

Their discovery of the abandoned greenhouse was more luck than judgement. At first, no one even recognised it as a greenhouse beneath the hardened grime on its presumably glass panels and steel frame. It was like no building they had seen before; inside it, someone had built stone walls which divided the space into several narrow paths. But they did not concern themselves with its purpose; it was just the remnants of the people who'd left Earth long ago – something they hadn't been able to take with them.

Most of their duties entailed verifying and comparing the present conditions on Earth to records from the pre-disaster era. The crew discussed their observations at length, gathered measurements and evidence, came to conclusions. Whenever they landed, the sights seemed much the same: clusters of spear-like plants ascending through the downpour; stones rounded and hollowed out by the endless fall of rain; statues with vanished faces, columns with their weatherworn reliefs. Long before they could conclude whether life on Earth might be possible again, they were finding traces of the people who had once lived here and, more often, coming across the plants that had overgrown them.

But it was hard to confirm and keep track of their discoveries. They were unsure what information they should include and what to delete. What would prove a success? What would be judged a mistake? No one could be sure. They knew from experience how easily their findings could be erased. It was why they left so many blanks in their official logs and records.

\*

Q was the first to take an interest in the greenhouse. There were a lot of them in disuse or in ruins in that area. This one looked something like a botanical garden. He collected seeds from the different species of wild plants that grew around the greenhouse and started planting them inside.

At first, everyone thought it was just a hobby, something to pass the time. That's right – none of us thought it would become an experiment. I don't think even he saw what he was doing as an experiment. The crew members tried to help where they could, removing the grime from the greenhouse exterior, repairing the artificial lights, getting the thermostat up and running again, constructing a ventilator.

There were some early teething issues, though once they got the conditions right, the plants grew very quickly. Everyone was delighted by that. The team had grown listless and disaffected and that small success brought them a much-needed sense of accomplishment. Soon enough, it became a competition for them.

No, I didn't take part. The plants didn't need my help, and the gardening seemed like nothing more than escapism. When we bumped into each other, I asked my colleagues how it was going, but only to be friendly, nothing else.

But their cultivation efforts never yielded any results, not a single fruit or flower; even though the expedition seemed long to us, it never lasted more than two of Earth's four seasons. In the fierce heat of Earth's dry season, people tired more easily and machines quickly overheated. So, although the team often proposed exploring during the dry season, their plans were routinely dismissed, which meant that the missions always took place in the rainy seasons.

Though we landed in a slightly different location every time, the team never failed to pay a visit to the large greenhouse. Q would go in first to inspect the damage. No one followed him in; they still remembered the first time we returned to the greenhouse and found it full of rotted-black leaves, sagging branches, desiccated grass and the stench of decay.

It was always the same. The dry air from the artificial lights, the extremely high concentration of oxygen, completely different conditions from those of the wild plants. Maybe this is a poor choice of words, but it looked like they had suffocated.

Q cleaned up the greenhouse alone. He uprooted the dead plants, evened out the soil, inspected the lighting and thermostat settings, and made plans to start anew. He planted all the seeds again in the cleaned-up greenhouse and tended them lovingly. As though nothing had happened. Only then, once the plants had grown back to a certain point, the rest of the crew would start visiting the greenhouse again. This cycle repeated itself on every subsequent expedition, the same process over and over. To me, it looked like he was fostering them only to kill them, and killing them to grow them all over again.

*

When the recovery team arrived to transport them off Earth, the crew was in better shape than had been reported. They had rationed the remaining food and been careful with their resources. Though tired and fairly hungry, everyone seemed in good health.

The recovery went smoothly and soon, they re-embarked on the space shuttle heading back to the Union. The return flight was the smoothest they had been on. The biggest jolt was receiving the news from the Union. During their first meal, they heard that public opinion was coming around to the return project throughout the Interplanetary Union. It had come out that research centre executives had greatly downplayed the findings from the first expedition and had decided that people returning to Earth was against the interests of the research centre. Now that this information had leaked, a full-scale investigation was being launched into the entire project.

On nights when he couldn't sleep, G went out to the empty lounge and watched the Union's press video looping over and over again. He knew it almost by heart. In order to breathe in outer space, you need an air tank calibrated to the atmospheric conditions you had become accustomed to. Neither Q or G could breathe the same air as anyone else in the expedition team, the air inside G's tank a similar composition to the air on Earth.

G thought of the plants Q had left to die, the spare flowerpots always in the greenhouse. Whenever he was about to leave it, G secretly took off his helmet. Cool air kissed his skin. He felt as if his bones were clicking into place. Rain fell and beaded on the tip of his nose, then rolled off. There was the endless sound of white noise and the strong, fishy smell of grass. It was a scent he could pick up even with his underdeveloped sense of smell. Whenever he caught a whiff of it, G knew exactly where he was.

He reached up and felt around his face. His fingers touched damp skin. A novel sensation. He began to feel a little breathless. Soon he would start to hyperventilate and become unable to catch his breath. G began to pant. You alright? Someone was talking to him. He quickly slipped his helmet back on. But the person was already beside him. G couldn't see the way their face, obscured behind their respirator, crumpled.

\*

Is he really dead? No one ever found his body. All we were told was that he went missing and has not been located yet. Maybe he's somewhere living on Earth. He believed so deeply that humans could make the return. I know the two of us fought constantly, but he was a capable scientist and a talented engineer. Knowing him, he'd probably find a way to adapt to life on Earth again.

*

Not long after they left Earth, the crew received word of a recovery team on its way to find a person who had been left behind. A commercial space airline had even provided the shuttle. Rescue efforts centred on the greenhouse, the last place he had been seen. The plants he had tended glowed a lush green, rich and vibrant, an image the recovery team transmitted to every corner of every city in the Interplanetary Union. A thorough search of the site was carried out but turned up nothing other than smashed flowerpots. The shape of their fragments suggested they had been destroyed in a powerful collision. All the while, the plants were pumping out endless streams of rich and deadly oxygen.

# Imperfect Pitch

His walks have become less and less frequent. He used to take them five times a week, which has shrunk to three, and now there are many days he doesn't leave the house at all. It is as if the walks require too much mental energy. Now, instead of going out, he sits at his computer, reading posts on an online message board. At work, his lunch break isn't long enough for much else. With the smell of food lingering in the office, he clicks through several pages before ending up back at the first, where a few new posts have appeared. Which, of course, he reads too.

His phone buzzes. A message from one of his group chats. He's going on a trip with some friends in a few weeks. He takes his eyes off the monitor for a brief second and scans the message. They're asking him to choose where they should stay and have sent along a bunch of pictures of places with similar layouts and colour schemes, each with equally well-proportioned beds, desks, closets, etc. And pictures of the beach. All the hotels boast gorgeous views. Baek glances through the photos and says that he'll go with whatever the rest of the group decides. And, with that, he returns to the monitor.

*RIP.*

Lots of posts have similar titles.

*Such a shock.*

*Just the other day, I saw her posting here.*

He reads and re-reads the same posts, closes the tab, opens another and searches the message board again. The first page is filled with more and more of the same sort of messages.

It is O's sister who posts the news of her death.

*Hello. This is O's sister. Early this morning, my older sister passed away. While she was alive, she absolutely loved this band. I'm posting here because I thought she would have liked to receive the thoughts and prayers of members of this message board. Thank you.*

It's just a short post, and Baek reads it again and again. He thinks of O. But he doesn't know enough to think about her for long. O was always the first to upload news to the fancafe, would coordinate group purchases of the band's albums and merch now and then, and upload fan accounts from their concerts. She didn't post or comment much aside from her info posts, so it was hard to guess what she'd been like. Even though she logged in every day to share news with other fans, she had been averse to meeting or contacting them directly. It was rare for anyone to comment on O's posts, but everyone knew it was because of people like her that the fancafe for a foreign rock band – a long way past its prime, at that – had managed to stay so active.

*

Baek met O at the venue where Imperfect Pitch had played their last concert. The group had decided to disband in the wake of sexual assault allegations made against one of the members, accused of slipping a date rape drug to a girl in a club. The girl in question named the band's guitarist in an interview six months after the incident, and the case was all over the news.

The fanclub members couldn't understand why it had taken so long for the girl to come forward. As soon as the allegations went public, some people said they would leave the fancafe although it seemed there was no notable impact on the membership numbers. All that happened was the daily number of posts decreased sharply. While the fancafe members were careful not to rush to comment, the number of news and information posts remained steady. Which was all thanks to O.

O was the first to post the news of the group's split. She also shared updates on the charges against the guitarist and, later, developments in his ongoing trial. She was the first to share the subsequent statement from the group.

*We're sorry to have caused you all concern recently with the unfortunate news regarding P. After consulting with our management and the other members, P has decided to leave the group of his own volition. Moreover, in accordance with the band's reluctance to continue with fewer than four members, Imperfect Pitch will disband permanently in the spring of next year.*

A moment later, a new post went up: an announcement of one final concert before the group's disbandment. O kept it brief, adding: *As soon as information on the specific date and time becomes available, I will upload it here.*

Naturally, this prompted a huge spike in traffic on the open forum. Lots of threads appeared, opinions ranging from people who felt gratitude for the final concert to others who thought it better for the band to disappear quietly. Someone posted the question: *Then who'll play the guitar?* O, who rarely appeared on the open forums, commented in a reply that another band's guitarist would be filling in. *In which case, can't they just add that guitarist to the band's permanent line-up?*

someone suggested, which provoked much agreement, although that was where the discussion ended. Without knowing any further details about the concert, all they could do was abstain from adding to the cacophony of hearsay and rumour around the band.

Until O came back several days later with information about the concert, no one else posted anything else. Baek still checked the site often, reading and re-reading posts and comments, though less out of a genuine interest than the weight of something like compulsion.

One single farewell concert was announced in the band's hometown, a two-hour flight away.

*The venue is pretty big. If you have a credit card that works overseas, I'd say it's worth trying to go. I'm definitely planning to. Anyone else here going?*

Underneath, a long string of comments: *I want to go, but … Would I need the tickets to be forwarded to me there? Anyone know a ticket site that's selling them? Can I get the tickets delivered to a hotel there?* Baek read each one before scrolling back to the top, even though he had no interest in it all.

That evening, he looked for his Imperfect Pitch album, which naturally, he couldn't find despite being certain it was in his house somewhere – probably lost in a move at some point – so he had no choice but to stream it. He turned on his Bluetooth speaker at his desk and listened to the album with the volume low. Then, before 11 o'clock, he switched it off and got into bed.

Baek could not say why he liked them so much. It wasn't as if the lead singer had exceptional vocals, or their melodies were that original, or they were that technically gifted. He couldn't even be sure what their genre was. Maybe he didn't actually like them. Maybe it was simply that Imperfect Pitch had made the songs he listened to the most, and whenever someone asked about his music tastes, the first name that came to mind was theirs.

*

Baek discovered Imperfect Pitch in his first year of university. Out of all the clubs and societies, he chose to join the music club. It wasn't that he had a particular passion for music; he didn't know how to read music or play an instrument, had no special preference for any particular bands, artists or genres. He mostly listened to songs on the radio which, overall, he was happy with. He joined the band because the first friends he'd made were in it and he wanted to keep with them.

When the second-years in charge of the club were recruiting first-years to join, they asked if Baek and his friends would be around to put on a performance that summer. Yes, they said.

Baek planned to perform a couple of songs he knew, along with an unfamiliar song: 'Ophelia' by Imperfect Pitch. The song was the band's first single. They'd recorded it at the guitarist's house on home studio equipment with very few copies made. Still, because they never became that popular, even this rare single wasn't that hard to get hold of. One of the second-years who had been so keen to hear 'Ophelia' already owned two pristine secondhand copies.

It was him who gave Baek the address for the band's fancafe site, in order to get the music tabs for their songs. When Baek told him he didn't know how to read music, the second-year said he'd have to learn if he wanted to perform together. As soon as he was home again, Baek found the fancafe online and applied to join. Within minutes, he saw his request was accepted.

Baek had never played guitar before – everyone's role in the band was decided by nothing more rational than a game of rock, paper, scissors. The second-years spoke passionately about the importance of using open strings, moving between chords seamlessly, dexterity exercises, the chromatic scale, and so on, but Baek studied nothing except for where to put his fingers for each song. Although it hurt his fingertips, he found playing easy enough to pick up. After their final exams, they practised and went out drinking afterwards, every day for two weeks.

On his way to each rehearsal and afterwards, going drunkenly home, he listened to Imperfect Pitch's first album on repeat as one of the second-years had said even listening was practice. Baek had never really listened to whole albums from beginning to end, but he was dedicated to his new pursuit and listened to the album religiously. The second-year who'd first recommended the band told him he was doing well and Baek practised even harder.

Now and then, when he was on the bus, he would pause the album and go to the fancafe site on his phone. In just a single day there'd be several pages of posts on the message board: *Where is everyone based? I'm listening to IP at work today and feeling pretty good. I gave a friend the CD today. I'm putting together the music tabs for the new songs – has anyone here figured out the chords?* None of the posts were intended to start a real conversation.

Baek usually woke around 7 o'clock. The first thing he did when he opened his eyes was check his email. Usually he'd have anywhere from five to twenty work emails and a ton of spam. He read, deleted, and labelled them over breakfast. Then he headed out, crossed the park to get to the bus stop, where he caught the bus to work. All morning, he responded to inquiries, fulfilled orders, and gave appropriate instruction on things that needed clarifying. His job involved writing code for the firm's clients. He would work for about three hours, then have lunch with his coworkers, sometimes with coffee after. After lunch he'd have a light walk and then return to the office. Once he got off work, he almost never ate dinner, just threw back beer and nuts with the news. And throughout his day, at all hours in fact, wherever he was he'd be reading old fancafe posts on his phone.

*My friend ended up not being able to go to the concert – would anybody want to buy her ticket off me?* A recent post from O. *Please message if you're interested.*

There were already quite a few comments. Baek checked his phone calendar. The date fell right after the deadline for his current project – a good time for a short trip.

On impulse, he looked up plane tickets online. The flights were affordable, and after a few clicks, he got an email: his ticket had been booked. He re-opened O's post. There were even more comments. Baek direct messaged O, then saw that his bus stop was coming up. He got off in front of the park and was walking home when he checked his phone again and saw a reply from O. *Someone got in touch before you. Sorry.*

He made a mental note to cancel the flight as soon as he got home.

He showered, had a beer and some nuts, and watched the news. He turned on the computer and browsed for clothes on a shopping site, then turned it off again. It was only as he was brushing his teeth that he remembered he'd meant to cancel the flight. He looked back at the black monitor screen. He would have to check how much the cancellation fee was. If it was too much, he thought, maybe he would go anyway.

Yet he quickly thought better of it – he wasn't the travelling type. Just considering the disturbance to his routine was stressful. Cancelling would be simple, he thought, all he had to do was switch on the computer, go to the airline's website and, in a couple clicks, he'd be done. If turning it on was too much effort, he could even do it on his phone. There was still time. He looked at the clock. 11:07. Baek set the alarm on his phone. It was time for bed – he would cancel the flight tomorrow.

But he didn't cancel it the next day, either. It was after he'd finished work and turned off the computer that he remembered. And somehow turning the computer back on seemed like too much effort. Nor did he want to hunt around for the cancel button on his tiny phone screen.

Some days later, he saw another private message from O. The person she was going to transfer the ticket to hadn't replied to her: *Are you still interested?* Baek hesitated. He thought of the flight he hadn't cancelled.

Another message from O: *If you are, please reply within 10 minutes.*

It had been about four minutes since the first message.

With three minutes still to go, he replied to her.

She got back right away. *You can just wire me the cost of the ticket.*

Below was her real name, he imagined, and her bank account number. He'd come across at least one person in every year of school with the same name. He wired the money over right away and messaged her to confirm. *Yes, I got it. I'll get the ticket to you on the day of the show.*

Nothing else from her after that although he waited for about an hour with his inbox open.

Only then did Baek think about the amount of money he had transferred, not to mention the cost of the plane ticket. Maybe O didn't even have a ticket to sell. He wondered if there was a way to see reviews from people who'd done transactions with O in the past. He read through all the fancafe posts that mentioned her. Most were thanking her. For sharing new info, for some hard-to-find merch, for holding a giveaway, for the link to an overseas auction site – everyone thanking her, followed by her polite replies. There was very little that could be inferred from these posts. Baek closed the browser.

*

Everyone returns to the office from their post-lunch coffee breaks, and Baek opens up the code he was working on earlier. The cursor is blinking but he can hardly focus. He thinks he has indigestion – probably sitting at the computer with such poor posture. He gets up and stretches. He's rifling through his drawers for antacids when he sees an in-office message window flashing in the corner of his screen.

He attends a meeting in which no one says anything much. Delivery dates may be pushed forward slightly because their partner companies are bogged down with other expenses, but they've been talking about this for weeks now. I know it'll be tough, the boss says, but do you think we can move up our deadlines?

It's not really a question.

The meeting over, Baek returns to his desk.

In the short time he's been away, his inbox has filled with new messages. He clicks it open – then closes it right away. He puts his phone down beside his keyboard. Everyone around him is busy, and Baek takes a moment to open the fancafe page. Most of the messages are still memorials for O. Baek has read all of them several times already, but he starts at the top and reads them over again.

For several days he's like this, unable to focus, logging onto the fancafe all the time, even at work. He can't use the office wi-fi so has no choice but to use his phone's data. He tries to limit how long he spends on his phone but finds himself anxiously refreshing the screen. But there are hardly any new posts. He figures everyone is still thinking about O's death.

He's on the forums on his way home too. As there are rarely any new posts, he re-reads old ones again. He feels slightly motion sick, but it's not too bad. With no new posts or even comments, Baek starts to feel slightly alone. And all things considered, he's alright with that.

After days without any updates, he comes across a post that begins: *I'm thinking of going to pay my respects to O…* Its author asks if anyone on the forum had been in touch with O personally. Baek can't help but think of the messages he and O exchanged a few months earlier. O's real name. The details that she sent. Facts that reveal nothing. After the concert, Baek had messaged O. *Thank you for the ticket. I had a great time at the show thanks to you. I'd like to treat you to a meal to show my appreciation, if that's alright?*

But O politely turned him down. *Just your thanks is fine.*

Baek imagines she'd have been as demure and distant with the post he's just read. He scrolls down. Still no comments, just a rising number of people viewing it.

There are still no replies when its author adds: *Is there really no one here who was close to O? I'd imagine there'd be at least one of us. If you don't want to comment here, you can message instead.*

The author updates the post again a couple hours later: *Seriously, how come no one's contacted me?*

Then beneath that someone else comments: *I've been around since back when O was the manager of this site. I don't think she would have liked this.*

Baek has never seen this username before. He looks it up. But he can't find any trace of activity from the user in question.

The number of views on the post is soaring; there are more than a few people like Baek out there, refreshing the page, eyes glued to the screen, waiting expectantly for someone else to comment, hoping for some progress.

*I read your posts, and I think this feels a bit much. And to be real with you, how do you know if that person really is O's sister?* Another comment. Yet another unfamiliar username. Baek clicks on it and a warning dialogue box pops up. *This comment does not exist.* The screen refreshes and takes him back to the first page. Baek finds the post he was just reading. The number of comments hasn't changed though the number of views has soared. The comment he just saw is gone. Baek taps the refresh button again and again. But no one has anything more to say.

*

He had a dream that he was playing hide-and-seek in an old hotel on the beach. The hotel had a long corridor. All the doors were identical, running in an endless line down the hallway. Their metalwork rusty, the numbers peeling. He opened each of the doors one by one. All the rooms were the same: a desk and chair, a TV and fridge, faded curtains, bedding that had been ironed smooth. A bathroom with ivory tiles. Underneath the blankets, behind the curtains, inside the cabinet and, hiding at the back of the closet, black crouching things. They were the people Baek was trying to find. Baek opened the closet doors, looked behind the curtains, moved the bookshelves aside. They weren't even hiding very well. People with dark bodies and erased faces. *Beware,* came voices but Baek wanted to see their faces. All he could hear were their voices, familiar, distinct. *Beware.*

When he awoke, feeling someone was talking to him, it was time for his in-flight meal. He chose a Chinese-style chicken and rice meal. But aside from a few pieces of chicken and a bread roll, he left it untouched. He felt restless. He couldn't tell if it was because he'd woken up at an unaccustomed hour or if it was the ton of coffee he'd had. Or maybe it was all the stuff he'd been carrying, or the dream he'd just woken up from. He dismissed each reason as it occurred to him.

In the queue at border control, Baek was unsure whether or not to message O. If he was going to get the ticket from her, he'd need to know what she looked like. Baek didn't know if she'd even made it here. And his queue wasn't moving. He looked around at the crowds of people packed in there. Why did it always have to be this stressful? Just as he made it to the gate the signs showed: FINAL BOARDING CALL. He was one of the last on the plane. He hauled along his suitcase, bumping people's legs in the aisle, his seat almost at the back of the plane. As soon as he sat down, he fell asleep.

It was getting off the plane that he started to feel dizzy, thinking at first it might be the effects of his travel sickness medicine. He looked around as he was swept towards border control. Unfamiliar words everywhere. It seemed the airport didn't have free wi-fi. Clutching his phone, Baek went through immigration, found his luggage, and bought a SIM card. His suitcase rattled over bumps.

Getting on the train into town, he messaged O: *Hello. This is the person who bought your concert ticket. What would be the best way to pick it up?*

But O didn't answer. Baek kept unlocking his phone, checking the fancafe message board, listening to the announcements on the train, studying the map on his phone. O still hadn't answered, and his battery was draining rapidly.

He was sitting in a cafe near the concert venue when O finally messaged. *There are lockers in the subway station. You can open them with a passcode. I've left the ticket in locker 892. The passcode is 4972.*

Baek read over the message slowly. A moment later, another one came. *Locker 892 is near Exit C.*

He looked out the window. The subway station was just a stone's throw from the cafe. He grabbed his coffee and headed off. Presented with so many entrances to the station, he decided to go into the nearest one. But even then, surrounded by so many people, it was hard for him to find his way.

However, just as O had said, he found the lockers near Exit C. Locker 892 was in the third row down, fifth one from the left, slightly below eye level. Baek entered the numbers on the keypad. 4, 9, 7, 2. He heard the metal gears shifting. The locker opened. There was a stiff piece of paper inside. *Imperfect Pitch: The Very Last Moment.* His seat was in section B, row 85.

Just then, his phone buzzed. O's username flashed on the screen. *Did you find the ticket alright?*

Baek looked around. She might have been any one of the people roaming around near the lockers, hiding behind a column, peering over her sunglasses in one of the fast food spots in the station. In the midst of the chaos, he heard a bell. Another train arriving. Baek could see people crowding and pushing their way to the platform. It was at that moment that he locked eyes with someone – he peered after them but they were immediately lost in the crowd, amid more people coming up the stairs and flooding the already crammed station. Baek peered among them but couldn't see the person anywhere. His phone buzzed again, the unanswered message flashing once more.

Baek tapped out a slow reply: *Yes, I just found it. Thank you.*

A moment later came a reply from O. *That's a relief. Enjoy the show.*

Baek didn't know if he should respond, if the person he'd locked eyes with was who he thought it was. He put his phone in his bag and clutched the ticket; although it was stiff, it felt light.

There was still time until the concert. O was clearly somewhere around and Baek wanted to find her. He started walking.

*

Baek's performance was at a small club near the university campus. They had been getting ready for days – the second-years checking the sound equipment and lights, the first-years in charge of the food and the flyers. Baek's group was doing promotion, texting alumni and going around sticking bright-coloured arrows on the ground. They were all chatty and vivacious, the air around them rippling with anticipation.

Aren't you nervous? one of them asked.

Not a bit, one guy said, I was in a band at high school.

Still, everybody gets nervous, someone else said, have you practised much?

More than you, the other one replied.

One guy beside Baek clapped him on the shoulder. Why are you so spaced out? he asked. It's too hot outside, said Baek and, true, the sun *was* blazing down on them – the back of his neck scalding in the heat – though, maybe it was more because this was their last rehearsal before the show.

Back at the concert venue, the engineers in the booth were testing the lights and all the sound channels. In the corner, Baek was trying to remember the songs. He felt another wave of nausea, the snacks he'd had earlier threatening to come back up, unable all of a sudden to remember the setlist or even how to play the songs. He was bewildered by the flickering lights; every time some- one plugged in a different cable all he heard was crackling static noise. The first band was already on stage, full of laughter as they did their sound check. Baek wanted to go home. Other people's voices seemed suddenly strange to him. There was the noise of the amp being plugged in.

Then it was Baek's turn. One of his bandmates handed him the guitar and made a joke. Baek forced his face into a smile. One of the second-years patted him on the shoulder. The guitar felt incredibly heavy. A bandmate held out a plastic bag from the convenience store filled with canned coffees.

*

Baek downed the rest of his coffee, took his tray and got up. Burgers were light, easy fare – you could eat them anywhere. Binning his rubbish, he looked out the window and noticed it was drizzling. People coming up the stairs were slick with rain. He had an umbrella back at the hotel and, as the fast food place was connected to the subway station, he could still go back, grab it and return without getting wet.

But Baek was exhausted. After countless cups of coffee he didn't want to move another muscle. He regretted getting rid of the bag he'd bought the burgers in. But, seeing no other option, he went back downstairs and ordered yet another soft drink. Returning, he found someone else had taken his seat and so headed towards the long table by the window. But its long plastic bench looked so uncomfortable that instead he squeezed himself between a group of people already sat down. His leg hurt. Sat directly beside a staircase and all the people travelling up and down, incomprehensible words passing in and out of his ears, though he could make out some talking about Imperfect Pitch. He wanted to hear something familiar and put his earbuds in. Although he immediately pulled them out again – he couldn't hear the music over everyone's noise. All their dispassionate faces made him anxious. It felt like the shells around their words were breaking open.

Baek took his ticket out of his bag and looked at it again. He wondered if it might be fake. The stiff, white paper, the words printed on it, the unintelligible fine print. Baek wondered how normal it was to get tickets to a final show so near the retail price; he wasn't a regular concertgoer and didn't know the going rate for touted tickets.

It took him ages to get into the venue, as if all the people in the fast food place were now here in line for the show. Although the rain had stopped, it had grown cold outside. Baek shivered, unsure whether he'd stay here or just go back to the hotel. He was desperate to get out of the queue. But there were too many people crowded around him. Imagining the effort it'd take to get through them, all the apologies he'd have to give, the faces he'd have to encounter as he pushed between them, he allowed himself to flood forward with them all.

Inside the venue at last, he looked around. O had to be in there somewhere. Maybe the person sat right next to him? No, all the people around him were locals. Where could she be? He considered the little he knew about her; she was always the first to know what was going on; she'd sold him one of her concert tickets, a decent seat too. And there was her bank account number and username on the fancafe, as well as her incredibly common first name. That was all.

The concert wasn't bad. Section B, row 85, was relatively close to the stage. There was a foreigner sitting in front of him and although he was at least 6' 2" and partially obscuring the view, Baek found he didn't mind at all. He just watched the big screens instead. The camera mostly focused on the lead singer, only occasionally showing the other band members. When Baek looked at the stage, all he could see clearly were their trainers.

Baek sang along with everyone at the songs he knew. It should have been fun. Yet he found himself wanting it to end. He threw himself into singing and dancing to try and overcome it. But when the band played one of their newer songs, Baek could only stare blankly at the big screens; even though he'd listened to all their albums beforehand, there were still songs he didn't quite know, which left him awkwardly waving his hands along with the crowd, mumbling the lyrics. When he lost the rhythm, his hands brushed those of the people near him and he wished the band would hurry up and launch into the next song.

The last song of the night was 'Ophelia'.

*

All in all, the rehearsal went fine. Baek couldn't believe he'd managed to get through it without a single mistake. Guitar still on his shoulder, he wiped his sweating palms on his trousers. Everyone was full of congratulation – *nice work, good job* – which made him feel he should keep the guitar on. You looked nervous, one of the second-years said, but everyone's nervous first time out.

Baek hardly acknowledged him. Around them, the crew were clearing away the canned coffees.

The show itself was due to start in a short while and people were already filing in – department alumni, friends and partners, other seniors, though not enough to fill the hall. Baek greeted them. For a while it grew noisier, and then the lights went dark. The spotlights came on, grew larger. Baek and the others stood under the stage as the first band went on, looking flushed.

That familiar intro, the same guitar riff over and over, the drums scattering before the bass comes in and the lead singer starts: Ophelia, I didn't call your name, I didn't hear your voice. Baek had the strange feeling there was something wrong with the sound. Over the tall guy's shoulders, he studied the band members. Their hands appeared to move in time to the music, but Baek couldn't be sure. Beside him, people sang along, danced, waved their hands, cheered. But, for Baek, every moment of that concert moved excruciatingly slowly.

Even though the band were stood in the same place, he couldn't hear their instruments. Maybe it was the speakers. Usually when he practised, he didn't listen closely to the instruments around him but took assurance from their sound. Now, though, chewing his lip, he realised his guitar solo was coming up. It hadn't been in the original song and he wished now he'd written it down and learned it instead of just remembering the hand positions.

The crowd was so loud they drowned out the singer, an odd wave of discordance running through the venue. With nothing he could hold onto, Baek's fingers grasped at the air. He looked around. Now the guitar and the bass were playing completely different notes. Surely everyone could hear it. Baek thought of O. But she wasn't there. It was only him in the crowd experiencing this, he felt.

For the briefest moment, the mic went dead. On the big screens, the lead singer had his mouth wide open. All the crowd could hear were the instruments and their own singing when, out of nowhere, there came a piercing screech. The audience went quiet and covered their ears. The singer's shocked face filled the screens, his eyes wide, looking back at an audience that could no longer hear him. The lights suddenly went out and all the instruments fell silent.

It was almost time. Baek readied his hands on the guitar's strings – his fingers aching, ears ringing. He couldn't hear the lead singer, couldn't hear anything. There was no way he could play this. But everyone else seemed fine. The lead singer turned towards him and smiled, the bassist's fingers flying. But Baek still couldn't hear a thing. He began moving his own fingers, certain he was making a mistake. He couldn't remember who'd told him he could do this. He watched the singer grip the mic.

Baek and the band bowed to the crowd and left the stage. His fingertips were sore, and he felt his legs shaking. But his steps had never been more measured, more assured. Other bands were up after them. Someone spoke to Baek, but he couldn't take in what they were saying. The place was full of noise. All these people mouthing words at one another, words that turned to nothing but sound. One of the second-years offered him a drink. As he sipped it, Baek resolved that, no matter what, he needed to avoid the after-party. He looked over at his bandmates laughing.

*Once I throw up, I'll feel better.*

Returning from the toilet, he couldn't tell which glass was his.

*Once I throw up, I'll feel better.*

It was something you only said when you were completely wasted, and Baek wasn't drunk at all. In fact, the more he drank, the more sober he felt. Even after getting out of the after-party, he found himself in the middle of it, at a huge table in a basement pub, drinking beer after beer in an attempt to find a lost sense of jollity.

He drank whatever people put in front of him, handed out drinks to others too. The music fluctuated, loud and quiet and loud again. Now it was a pop song someone was yelling along to. Baek's whole head was ringing. Stop the music, he wanted to say. But more and more people were singing along to it. He wanted to ask what had happened on stage, but the singing didn't let up. Someone sang as he filled Baek's cup. The song changed suddenly but the singing went on. And then, hesitantly at first, Baek started to sing along too. He felt someone's damp hand in his. Baek heard his voice grow louder and louder and watched himself knock over his beer.

\*

Back at the hotel, Baek logged onto the fancafe. Naturally, O had been the first to put up the band's final message. *Since the day we formed, we haven't ever played a perfect note.* It was a long post, and he scrolled down absentmindedly – no comments yet. He opened a new window and looked up O's username.

It was just a combination of her initials and birthday, all of it so common it wasn't easy to find her. Baek found several posts on other blogs, but judging from the writing style, the posts didn't seem to be O's. Searching for her real name only brought up information about lots of other people with the same name – people who'd bought and sold things on a secondhand marketplace, booked an appointment at a makeup studio for graduation photos, sought advice on how to finish the homework that had sat untouched all break, asked for recommendations on where to get their graduation pictures touched up. There was a page advertising insurance, and one complaining about a lover who'd left. Baek read each one. His interest never wavered. Although there seemed to be an infinite number of posts *about* her, O herself was completely absent.

Baek enjoyed the following few days in the city. He had compiled several reviews he'd found online, mapped out his itinerary accordingly and stuck to the plan. He took lots of pictures and saved everything – his receipts, tickets, leaflets. On the flight home, he looked at all of them again and, contented, fell sound asleep, the flight home uninterrupted by turbulence or anything else.

*

Not long after the concert, Baek heard that a new group formed by the band's frontman A had recently released their first album, and the drummer had taken a position as a professor of applied music. Both of which Baek learned through O, reading her posts over and over again on the bus to work. It was good to see good news. People in the fancafe liked the news too. The band released a DVD and Blu-Ray of their last concert, and people uploaded pictures from it online. Baek swiped through all the near-identical photos. Any posts that mentioned the sound issues were quickly deleted by the moderators.

Soon, news about the group became less frequent. A's new band didn't get any real success, their album not even making the charts. The news of singer P's marriage was almost immediately followed by news of his divorce, and soon after, his name appeared on gossip sites attached to rumours of a suicide attempt. The guitarist was sentenced to prison. Baek ate, went to work, came home, went on walks, went to the toilet, fell asleep, all the while reading the international entertainment pieces full of misspelled names and incorrect personal details.

These days no one posts on the open forums. None of the community went to O's funeral, even though posts about her are still the top threads on the message boards. Baek checks hourly for new ones. Only the number of page views increases, one hit at a time. Which, when he notices, makes him feel deeply alone. Although, all things considered, he's alright with that.

Baek goes on holiday. Just a small trip with some friends. They go to a city famous for its beaches and museums, with clean swimming pools on every roof. While there, the plan is to take long naps, eat delicious food, and go swimming. Baek thinks he might even get lucky and meet someone. He boards the plane feeling rather optimistic, his heart light now he's got through the more demanding tasks he needed to finish. Maybe by the time he gets back, everything will be sorted out.

On holiday he laughs a lot, wanders a lot, lies on the sunbed at the resort and drinks cocktails, shops, and goes for walks on the beach. While his friends are preoccupied with shopping, he sometimes checks the fancafe. He doesn't think about how he quit the band after just a term, or about the second-year whose hand he'd drunkenly held and whom he dated for half a year before things petered out between them. That evening, he floats in the rooftop swimming pool. He gets out to go inside, and though his ears are waterlogged, the warm air soothes him.

And then there is a new post on the fancafe from O's username. *Hello. This is O's sister. I thought I wouldn't post again, but this situation is getting out of hand. I don't know how this happened, but for the last two days I've had people calling my phone saying they've been watching me. I've found it very upsetting. I'm not sure how you got my number, but I would appreciate it if you didn't contact me anymore. With the help of a cyber crime team, I've gathered the personal information of the individuals who've been calling – this is just to*

*let the people on this site know that if I am contacted*
*again, I plan to take appropriate legal action.*

There are no comments below it, the number of views simply ticks up in silence. Baek stares blankly at his phone. His friends ask him what he's looking at. It's nothing, he replies.

Baek looks on as they rummage through the wares at different street stalls, drink freshly-squeezed fruit juice, walk together, contented, along the beach. Such pretty scenes to watch. Baek takes some photos, then checks his phone again, although he sees nothing new there.

## Paper Cut

A wanted to run away. He thought long and hard about what he would need. If he could get hold of a list of all the possible crimes in the world, and the world's most intricate and detailed map, then he'd know what he was guilty of, and where he could hide when it was time.

He wondered exactly where a list of all the world's crimes and the world's most complex map might be, but he couldn't begin to guess. After much consideration, A went and blew all his money on the most expensive smartphone on the market, hoping that, if he trawled the internet long enough, he'd eventually find the most remote place on Earth. Maybe he'd read every criminal law compendium in the world.

He began to realise there'd be a limit to how far he could go, and that even if he could get his hands on all the criminal law compendiums in the world, he'd be unable to understand them. Searching for 'most remote place' or 'best place to hide' yielded nothing useful. So, as an interim measure, he bought the thickest blackout curtains available. He had wanted to buy a padlock for the outside of the door though realised he wouldn't be able to lock it once he was in.

With his thick blackout curtains covering the windows, A lay in bed, failing to sleep. Under his pillow, he kept a Stanley knife, a maths workbook, and his new smartphone. The air conditioner was on at its coldest setting. All he could do was keep his eyes shut and lie dead still. There was one thing he needed to be awake for, however – the imminent visit from the person he knew only as 'that man'.

The visit had been prearranged, and though A could have shouted at him to fuck off, he was conscious that it would be just another item on life's ever-lengthening list of wrongs.

And so, sure enough, it was not long before the doorbell started to ring incessantly. A rubbed his stiff, heavy, cold arms with his stiff, heavy, cold hands, and shouted at whoever it was outside, Who is it?

But no one answered and the doorbell kept on ringing. Scowling, A rushed to unlock the door before the bell could ring again.

The visitor bowed slightly, closed his paper umbrella and stepped inside. Dark drops of rain were dripping from his hat, a kind of crude paper fedora, and out from under a pair of paper shoes, a puddle of water was spreading. Also drenched were his paper coat and socks, and beads of rain hung from his fingernails. A watched as the visitor leaned his paper umbrella in the corner, peeled off his paper shoes and put them down very precisely, then came in and sat at A's desk. From beyond the still-open door, A could hear the rain falling. He closed it and came back to his guest. You want something to drink? he asked. But the paper man shook his head. A sat down on his bed.

Alright, said the paper man. Time to write your statement.

A asked, What am I supposed to write?

The paper man replied, Anything.

A shrugged and said, Well, that's no help. I've no idea what I should write.

But the paper man said nothing more and instead took out paper and pencils from his paper suitcase and put them down on the desk. These, at least, weren't soaked from the rain.

I'll stop by again in ten days, said the paper man. Try and have the statement ready by then.

A gave no response and the paper man got up then, slid into the paper shoes, picked up his paper umbrella and left.

More from negligence than defiance, A didn't write the statement. Leaving the paper and pencils where they were, he lay in bed instead, his eyes shut, the air conditioning up high, passing the time.

Although, of course, when the paper man returned, not a single word of A's statement had been written.

Wait, wait, listen, he said. The thing is, I can't really remember what happened, but I think when I tried writing it, I found so many spelling mistakes that I needed to find the Tipp-ex, though all I found was a biro. So I just kept crossing lots out. I genuinely thought I would fix it later, but when I sat down again I realised I didn't have a dictionary. Look, I only have the one book in the flat and that's a maths workbook. But I tried the best I could, I swear.

The paper man said nothing, pursing his paper lips.

Please, said A. I know it's messy, but you can still read it.

The paper man said nothing for a long time, and then, eventually said, Look! You crossed out everything you wrote. You might as well have written nothing. You crossed it out several times, too – it's like writing nothing three or four times.

What am I supposed to do? asked A. I even wrote on both sides. I thought my hand was going to fall off!

The paper man sighed. I don't care if your fingers or toes fall off, there's nothing written here. I'm leaving more paper. It would be good if you wrote a statement I could read. Describe your innocence. Give your alibi. Attest. Whatever you think best. I'll let you borrow my Tipp-ex and my dictionary.

The paper man stood up. I'll be back in ten days.

Still A did not write the statement. He poured coffee and grape juice and nail polish remover on the paper. He imagined showing them to the paper man. Look at these stains! Do you think an official document like this would still be valid if it's so messy?

A crumpled up and tossed the rest of the paper under the bed. He destroyed the dictionary by hurling it at the wall repeatedly, then took the pages that had fallen out from it and folded them into turtles and cranes, then he took the sheets of paper and folded those into bulls and cicadas, making a tiny menagerie by his bed. He proudly showed off his creations to the paper man, who – rather than admiring his handiwork – merely slammed down more paper and left.

Even one sentence is fine. Write your statement – just a sentence will do. Every time the paper man left with these words, placing another ream of paper on A's desk before leaving, calling out, I'll be back in ten days.

A tossed it all on the ground, scattering the sheets across the floor of his small apartment, walking on them, kicking them around, rolling on them, screwing them up, though it made no difference – he was submerged, irrevocably, in paper.

Even if he smeared his tears or snot or spit on the sheets, they'd have been no different to the paper man from the other stuff he'd thrown on them. He stood up suddenly and, with some paper stuck to the bottom of his foot, grabbed the Stanley knife. Sat at his desk, he plucked a sheet of paper off the floor and began to cut it up.

Ten days later, when the paper man opened A's door, he found the floor of the apartment covered in white confetti. Some of the shreds were triangular, others misshapen trapezoids, some as wide as a finger, others string-thin. The paper man bent down and scooped some up, the white, weightless scraps rustling in his hands. A called over from where he lay in bed, a thin blanket pulled all the way up over his head.

It wasn't me, A said. It was like this when I woke up. Can you leave me some thicker paper that won't rip so easily next time?

The paper man said nothing, dropped to the ground and shoved the scraps into his mouth, the confetti vanishing into his paper body. After he'd shovelled the last strands of shredded paper into his mouth, he opened his paper suitcase. Clean sheets of folded paper were packed inside. The paper man put the paper down on A's desk. Write the statement properly this time, he said. No more bullshit.

But ten days later, the piles of paper were stacked on the desk just as he'd left them.

Where's the statement? the paper man asked, raindrops falling from the brim of his paper fedora.

A's eyes were closed, the blanket bunched up at his feet. On the desk, he replied. If you look closely, you'll find it.

The paper man rummaged through the papers and finally found a collection of stapled pages at the very bottom. In the centre of the first page was a title – 'STATEMENT' – and beneath it, A's name.

The man picked up the papers and slowly examined them one sheet at a time. There were about fifteen pages in total, all crowded with mathematical numbers and expressions scribbled in several colours. There were graphs and sums crossed out and rewritten. The paper man pressed his hand against his forehead. What the hell is this? he asked. What does all of this mean?

It's my statement, A replied, not even opening his eyes. The title's written right there.

How can you call this a statement?

A slowly sat up in bed. It's a simple formula, he said. A method for finding the derivative of a differential equation, but I messed up a few times. Are you able to follow it, or is maths not your forte? I could try to explain it to you but truth be told, I'm bad at calculus. I don't know the first thing about differentials. But if I managed to figure it out, I'm sure you can, too.

A chuckled softly.

The paper man shook his head. This won't do.

A merely shrugged. This is all I know how to do, he said.

I'll say it one more time – write your statement properly. I'm not leaving until you do.

A got back in bed and closed his eyes.

The paper man stayed at A's apartment. A lay in bed as usual, eyes shut, curtains drawn, air conditioning on high, the papers fluttering from their stack. Now and then, the paper man left the house for a few days at a time, returning with another ream that he put on the desk. When the paper man was gone, A would slice into the stacks of paper. Bright white paper shreds heaped up under him.

When the paper man returned, his wet paper socks sticking to the paper on the floor, he opened his paper suitcase and took out all the statements he had been out collecting.

A couldn't believe all these people had obediently written their statements, and that the paper man read them all so thoroughly, crossing things out, putting asterisks next to others, poring over each one carefully before shoving it in his mouth and swallowing.

What did they write? A asked.

They are other people's statements, not mine, the paper man told him. Look, you're not even sleeping properly. Wouldn't writing something at least mean you got something done, anything? It doesn't even have to be your statement.

When the paper man was out, A sat at his desk and tried a pen instead of the Stanley knife. But there were so many, and all either too heavy or too light or the wrong colour or designed badly or didn't write well, and with the air conditioning his fingers were too cold to take off the caps or click the pens. He found he was writing a graph and the solution to a maths problem in several colours of ink. But after a while, he tossed his pen aside – maths proved to be as hard as writing a statement – and grabbed the knife again. Pushing out the blade of the Stanley knife was laughably easier than writing. Like a machine, A sliced cleanly through the paper.

The paper man's outings grew less frequent, the number of statements he returned with dropping from several dozen to a few. One day, he returned and announced, I've gathered almost all the statements I need.

A lay in bed, eyes closed. Yeah? he replied, indifferent.

Aside from one, the paper man said. Yours. Hurry up and write it. It's your duty.

But A pulled his blanket up higher and said, Why?

Because you're the only one who's still told me nothing. It's your responsibility to say something. And it's mine to collect it when you do. Come on, if you don't get up now I'll smother you with paper.

He waved the stack of papers menacingly, his paper feet kicking up a lethal cloud of paper dust.

Reluctantly, A got up and sat at his desk. His whole body was stiff, heavy, and cold. Give me some paper, he said.

The paper man handed him the stack. A began to write something. A while later, he put the pen down and handed over the paper to the paper man. As he read, his paper mouth twisted up.

Why won't you fucking write a statement?

This *is* my statement.

The paper man slapped it down on the desk. The pages were crammed with formulas and graphs, numbers and variables.

Write it again, the paper man said. He put a new stack of paper in front of him. A started writing but before he could even get to an equals sign, the paper man screamed and snatched the paper from him, tearing a hole in it, leaving a pen mark on the desk. He wiped away the mark with the palm of his hand and slammed a new stack of paper down. Write the statement. Write it properly. It's all you have to do.

When A started to draw a new graph, the paper man snatched the sheet from him again, leaving another mark on the desk.

Cut it out, the paper man roared. What sort of statement is this? What the hell are all these equations supposed to be?

The paper man tore A's problems to shreds. A looked on quietly as he howled and tossed the shredded bits of paper everywhere, raining confetti all over the floor. Then he began spewing paper – sheet after sheet flew out from the sleeves of his paper coat, from his paper socks, from the heels of his paper shoes, from his paper fedora.

Write your statement! You have to! Write it properly, now, right now, fast!

But A didn't write his statement. Instead, he shook off the paper dust and picked up the Stanley knife. Still shooting out paper, the paper man watched A slide the blade up with a krr-krr-krr noise, snap off the tip and toss away the old blade. Then he watched

A return to the desk and lower the fresh blade to the sheet. As he sliced through it, the paper came gushing from the paper man, falling to the floor as confetti, strings, dust.

A's movements were machine-like. He sliced and shifted, sliced and shifted, the new strands mingling with the mess of paper already on the ground. Above his head, the paper man shot a spate of paper, not even stopping when the blade nicked his skin and he started to bleed. Red confetti joined the white in the cramped apartment, and soon turned the colour of rust.

What the hell are you doing? shouted the paper man, his paper face trembling. Why the hell won't you write your statement?

Look, A said calmly, even in this story I'm not able to kill my parents. He kept slicing as he spoke. There's no real damage I could do with a Stanley knife. Nothing's ever gone right for me – I wasn't even able to hide away. Although now I can at least solve maths problems with differentials.

All the while, A did not stop cutting, the paper man shaking violently all over, unable to spit up any more paper. But A didn't notice, so focused was he. More blood spread on the paper, but A didn't stop. Up and down, side to side – until the last sheet of paper was torn to ribbons, then to dust.

A put the knife down on the desk. Even the chair now was buried under heaps of paper. The paper man took off his paper fedora and put it on the desk. His face crumpled pathetically.

All you had to do was write a statement, a few pages.

Did you really think that would make everything okay? said A. He picked up the paper man's paper hat and began to cut it up. The only person it would help is you.

The paper man's paper fedora was a heap of shredded bits in no time at all.

A took the paper man's hand in his, a dark red stain spreading over his white paper hand, and began to cut into it. He listened to the sound of the blade slicing through paper. The first to go were the paper man's paper fingernails. Next were the paper man's paper fingers. Then the paper man's paper palm and the paper back of his hand were lost to the blade. He cut up the paper man until his paper coat, paper cuffs, and paper shirt all turned to shreds.

Except for my maths workbook and you, that's all the paper I can see, A said. Still shredding, he added, Differentiation is the infinite dividing up of the space under a curve and the adding up of all of these sections. I still don't understand it. I can solve differential equations, but can't do calculus to save my life. Look at all the paper dust. A lungful of that and we'd both die. But you want a statement from me, something true?

The paper man didn't answer. A's blade was slicing into his paper vocal cords.

What happened to all the statements you swallowed? A asked, turning the paper man's paper lips to shreds. Where did you get all that paper from?

The paper man's paper chin was gone, then his paper throat, followed by his paper nose, paper eyelids, paper eyelashes. The paper man's paper chest and paper stomach disappeared. His paper thighs, paper knees, paper shins, paper ankles, and paper toes, his paper shoes and paper umbrella all became indistinguishable from the rest of the paper shreds and dust around.

A sat on the mound with the paper animals and thought. He still wanted to run away. He thought about the world's longest list of crimes, and the world's most intricate map. He could simply make the longest list of crimes by adding any new ones to the present list, the world's most intricate map by drawing in ever more minute detail on a current map. But neither would help him escape.

The rain hadn't let up. The room was full of the sound of raindrops hitting the window and the air conditioner unit running outside. A wanted to pool the rain to fill his apartment so that he might be able to escape. Maybe he would end up someplace without any calculus or written statements. But what was broken would stay broken, and what was destroyed he'd never be able to fix. A picked up a paper turtle and unfolded it, then the paper crane, the paper bull, and the paper cicada, all restored to sheets of paper. He picked up his maths workbook and began tearing off each page until it too was another pile of paper.

Then A picked up the knife.

## Failed Summer Vacation

I'd long been obsessed with the idea that I was pretending to be something other than myself, until the day I came to the realisation I'd never entirely been 'me' to begin with.

I'm not thinking about the ticket I left on the desk. I'm not thinking about the books I haven't even opened yet. Books with the most beautiful covers, filled with the ugliest stories. Some stories are best when you haven't read them, some movies most fascinating when all you've seen are their posters, the most terrifying curses the ones that hang over you forever, which is why I choose to wander through the days with books I'll never read and movies I'll never watch and—

I'd like to swallow glass shards. I'd pour them into a cup and watch the light reflect and refract through them. I'd pour cold water over them, pick up the cup and gulp down the shards like any ordinary drink. Their edges will slice my throat. Tiny scratches, omens of rupture, will accumulate, shredding my capillaries. I'll taste metal. Vessels and blood and plasma, white and red blood cells, iron and haemoglobin – all the things I once heard about in biology career through my head, and I am cheered at the thought of these glistening things – though they have no inherent lustre – destroying me from within. (Although none of this will happen. Before I even attempt to swallow them, my throat will reject them and I'll throw them up, the unfathomable machine of my muscles tightening and relaxing involuntarily.)

The days are repeating, blurring together so that I can't mark the end of any one with a full stop. They droop like a wet dough I've never been able to make into anything. I want to resist. To revolt. No listening to music, no drawing pictures, no talking. Absolutely no writing. There's a fish swimming around in the old bathtub. (I hope nothing is revealed from all these chaotic words.)

*

There is a definite permanence, or at least a sense of perpetuity, to a vacuum – I think about how painful it would feel to be inside one. When I was little, I saw on TV a marshmallow in a vacuum swelling until it burst. I feel I'm slowly coming apart, like stacks of wooden blocks wobbling at the slightest wind. I can't reveal the stacks that make up me unless I disguise or speculate about them, and as no one's ever come up with a good way to talk about pain, I have nothing to refer to. Sometimes it seems just how my brain's wired or how my muscles contract and expand excessively, or the minute fluctuations in my acid and alkali levels that mean when I suddenly hear a voice in the distance – unplaceable and fleeting – there is nothing there, just the sound of an unidentified liquid moving through my veins—

This room is tiny. Even at a glance, it looks poorly built. The floor is a misshapen triangle; the furniture appears to be crammed in almost forcibly. There are no windows and therefore no natural light. Just the table, wardrobe, bed, and my suitcase are enough to crowd the entire floor. Going into the bathroom, I am hit by the overpowering smell of bleach, though nothing here looks like it has been cleaned recently. I enter without slippers on. The tiles feel cool. The space between the soles of my feet and the grooves between the tiles I find unsettling. I climb into the bath tub, lie down and look up at the ceiling. The strange pattern on the tiles, the paint job and the exhaust fan are all the same jaundice-yellow.

I'd like to see the view, so I head out and upstairs. The green iron door to the rooftop is unlocked, and pulling or pushing it even a little makes it creak, which I enjoy – that sharp, grating sound that feels like my skin being ripped off. I look down at the street from the rooftop. This building stands in the heart of a residential area, and if I lean far enough over the railing, I can see people running up and down the side streets. They're all dressed differently, all of them releasing superfluous bodily fluids into the humid air. Heading down from the rooftop, I worry the stairs are so steep that I might take one wrong step and crack my head open.

These scenes that could easily vanish still haunt me. I open the door, filling the room with burning light. Everything weighs on me. I tiptoe towards the bed, trying not to think of poison. Some pain I can readily withstand. I sweep my fingers over the pillowcase, which rustles to the touch. When I lie down, I have the same dream as always: my body is present but my soul has escaped, and it's just the air, my sticky flesh, the humidity, the people running in the streets, all the carbon they're emitting and—

Each idea presses up against the next like skin on skin. My sweat runs against the grain of soft, standing hairs. Every molecule has heft. Stifled here under these frayed bedsheets on this rainy summer day, I'm perfectly able to stop myself thinking about curses, murder, death, hate, hostility, resentment—

This room is on the sixth floor of a fairly standard block of flats, and assuming each floor is around three metres in height, then I'm about fifteen metres off the ground, my eye level around seventeen metres up or, since I'm in bed, only fifteen metres. (Although my calculations maybe imprecise, a couple of metres at this height would probably not make the difference between life and death. I am too listless to map out my own demise exactly.)

I don't know what time you got here, but here you are, telling me we should go out. I sit up, my skin unsticking from itself with a wet sound. You say there's a beach nearby and, though I really don't want to move, I want to be gone from here, so I follow you out and down the steep staircase. The street is narrow and we walk like ghosts, forever untouching.

The streets are all identical and I worry we might get lost, but I don't want to spoil the holiday. A vacation you can't escape from isn't really a vacation, and haven't I been talking about a holiday for ages? I don't know what I'm so anxious about. I'd like to be as far away as possible from wherever I am – I don't want to interfere. I don't know what to do with you, what would be best. All I know is you are breathing, and the humidity, temperature, and density of your breath are swampy and menacing.

It's hard not to notice the difference in texture when foreign matter gets caught on an adhesive surface. I've never felt this sort of hostility before – stubby and soft and lumpishly round – I let it melt like caramel inside my mouth. I can even taste a sort of sweetness on my tongue. It's most delicious when you taste it only in your mind. The wind blows, hot and humid, and I see dark clouds in the distance. Sand comes scattering across the beach mat. You brush it off. You spot something and go and see what it is. A half-empty glass bottle topples and rolls over the sand. Although I can't see the label, I know it's the bottle you've just been drinking from.

Emotions, words, thoughts, air molecules, plastic scraps, the unhatched eggs of sea creatures, semi-conscious strands of seaweed strewn everywhere – you stride past them all, kicking as you go, sand filling your shoes with every step. When you take off your shoes you must feel a stinging at its sharp edges digging into your skin. You hold the shoes high and wobble where the sand gives way beneath you. To you, it feels soft and comforting and warm, even though I see thin cracks forming on your feet in the hot sun. It's impossible to tell the difference between the sand and finely ground glass.

Our first plan had been to go to a swimming pool today. I imagined it lined with bright blue tiles and cool, clean water flowing endlessly in and out. But somehow I've ended up in this rundown beach town, rolling your abandoned glass bottle on the sand. I imagine knocking the bottle over in the pool. Tomato juice would seep into the cool, blue water, which carries on moving, so the pool doesn't get cloudy, and I can float there on its frigid surface, looking up at the sky. No, the sun would be too bright. My damp hair, that chlorine smell, the bottle shards, my eyes stinging too much for me to hear the sound of anyone screaming. I want to shatter your glasses, crush your lips. I want to weaken the pull of your mouth, stop your breathing, sit beside the perfect rectangle of the pool forever and watch the water flowing and overflowing, its blue surface undisturbed. You'd be in red boxer shorts, I think. I'd lose a coloured contact lens in the pool then half cover my face with my stringy wet hair and turn to look at you with one black eye and one blue.

*

I will only ever write incorrect sentences, use all the wrong letters and the least suitable words. My slips and mistakes, my crooked handwriting and messy pages of crossings out and smears of colour, these I will let define me. The starkness of ink on paper, dark on light, will shape me.

An invisible barrier emerges. I want to be able to see both the micro and macroscopic at the same time, to see everything and so avoid all mistakes and any possible doubt. But there's always going to be mistakes and doubts: I'm the sort of person who'd dig a grave and then fall straight into it, a body with no coffin, ready for the worms. My dreams are always about failing. In one, I'm standing among the bodies of dead fish.

There's no need to dwell on all the chances I've missed. I don't believe in memory, don't trust it. I'll destroy the records, rip them up – I want to stretch the holes in the evidence, let in more misunderstandings like bubbles of air in ice. I will be explained solely through misunderstandings.

*

On the way back from the beach, we came across more runners moving as a single entity, limbs pumping together. Once they'd gone, you walked as though you'd walked this street all your life, as though you knew it like the back of your hand. I followed you in silence.

The neighbourhood is made up of several identical high walls, a maze with several dead ends and no clear way out. Perhaps intentionally, there is no way to chart it. After rounding several corners, we suddenly came across a row of drooping sunflowers. I had to stop myself from touching their drooping petals. We had only just made it back to the house when fat drops of rain began to fall. We climbed back up the steep staircase, the room still suffocatingly humid.

This cramped room. My alibi. Our freshly made beds. My thoughts roam wildly and I can't keep up. I think about grabbing one of the soft pillowcases, this one I'm holding now, or the thin scarf I haven't yet unpacked, and stuffing it in your mouth, no, tightening it around your neck. Although I am able to suppress or dismiss these urges, the things I want to say feel out of my control, predetermined even. I wish you great pain, I wish myself great pain, though my words don't stick. Instead I churn out familiar sentences as if nothing's the matter: it's all right, it's no big deal, I completely understand. However, certain words aren't in the dictionary, so I can't understand what I'm saying or the sentences I'm writing – for a long time I thought 'seditious' and 'sedulous' meant the same thing – and still you're talking about nearby places we should try, though this is nothing new.

We should go and eat something, you say.

We had planned to go to the swimming pool, though I guess it's the same cool water that comes from the sea of this rundown beach town, so maybe we've already accomplished our goal in a way—

How can I explain that all of this is not depression or just everyday disappointment? And why do I have to? My reasons are so flimsy they could be dispelled by a puff of wind. Shoulder to shoulder in this tiny place, dreaming of death or at least something like it. I don't really want to jump or drown. What I'd like instead is to fall without hitting the ground, to drown without taking on water. An odd curse to wish on yourself: to make it impossible to say if I've died or not. All this time you're focused only on walking. Behind you, I find myself strangely drawn towards building sites. And though this will go unnoticed or else be easily forgotten, it will remain, naked and indelible.

\*

Above all things, I'd love to be a traitor. I want to build up a legacy of betrayals, enough disillusionment that I would be crushed under it. I don't mind if the weight of it presses down on me slowly or slams into me all at once, I'd like to fail at being crushed to death, and after that failure I'd like to slit my wrists or leap off something or gouge out my eyes or mangle my fingers, though in the end it won't prove anything. Of course, that's not the point, I have nothing to prove to myself, but the absence of tangible evidence and my inability to show evidence even exists makes me anxious, glaring unblinking into the dark for a knife or a fizzing bomb to arrive, for the moment the poison spreads through my veins. Time congeals. A runny dough. Already stuck to your hands.

Our roles have been agreed on. We're prepared for all eventualities. For both of us. No one has picked up the knife yet. You sit up slowly and look around the dark room. At its crumpled interior. At me, my eyes closed, pretending I don't see you.

One moment will follow another until we get to the one in which we finally have to make a choice. The feel of your soundless footsteps. The door opening. It's strange but the creaky door hasn't made a peep all afternoon. There's no light leaking in behind you. It's so dark already. I open my eyes and you're gone.

The flimsiness of the alibi makes me uneasy, and so I tear up the receipts, stash my diaries, snap all the pens in the desk drawer, scratch out the names on all the business cards, and check you're gone before feeling around on the side table for the memo pad. A previous occupant has written at least one note. I can make out the faint impressions of pencil on paper. It's raining still. I can hear it falling: it's coming down hard. There must be a crack somewhere. I touch the wall, which is cool and perfectly dry, but I know I can't trust that dryness, that solidity.

Things of unknown whereabouts, things uncorroborated by evidence or witness – trying to talk about them like they're real can actually be painful, a sharpness in my airways like something scratching at the walls of tissue, which I can't reduce to some instinctive reaction of nerve or hormone or muscle. And because the words I have for explaining pain are imperfect, and because no one can feel another person's pain, I simply clamp my mouth shut and—

There's also the pain. Pain that works to alleviate pain; and the pain that comes from pain relieved. The world made clearer by obscuring things, the bright image in your eyes growing duller as you move away from the light. The heavy air in this room has suffused itself with an odd rage, and each time my lungs contract and expand, I end up breathing it in, but I want to know, don't want to know, can't know, don't know, want not to know, can't not know, want to hide where those things are coming from. I don't want to get caught so I'll pretend I have no suspicion or resentment or anxiety or rage, I'll conceal them, write new and never-ending alibis, leaving traces of falsehood on top of the traces of everything else. But they are everywhere, so even if I were to run down the steep staircase and out onto the street, their taint would probably still be all around—

I pull the blanket all the way up over my head. Soft, damp fabric wraps itself around my skin. The rain continues to fall and the wind, I think, has started blowing. I don't know why you went outside. My only guess might be to stir up some trouble we can get into.

I list all the opportunities I've been given and try weighing them against each other until each of them vanish, but there's always the kiss of one object touching another, the way you press on a pen, the strands of hair and dust, the missing witness and, honestly, thinking about all this is so exhausting that I just want to sleep but —

There was one time I got a bit of pencil lead stuck in my temple – as unbelievable as that sounds even to me – the doctor didn't remove it and my skin and body became swollen, though no one ever spoke about where it went or even about the mark on my temple, and now I'm feeling around the bedside in the dark, I can't find anything to help me sleep.

My hands on the rough texture of the pillowcase; thoughts I can't erase come to me one after another. The best way to remove traces of yourself is to leave false ones, and though I never learned how to compose an alibi, it came to me as easily as breathing, and now I can be here and not here, can plant the seeds of confusion just by muddling places and times. Tickets for a whole diaspora of destinations are spread out on my desk. I imagine my diaries ripped to shreds in some municipal paper shredder; diaries, I remember now, tearing apart with my own hands.

I hope no one comes after me, and that I can vanish amidst all my mismatched alibis, my corpse abandoned at a hospital somewhere, unclaimed by friends or family, stripped of organs, flesh peeled off, eyeballs removed, bones shattered, blood and bodily fluids all drained somewhere – if I disappear, please, don't look for me or try to help me. God, I hope it keeps raining. It would wash everything away perfectly, unless, as I fear, the waterways in this city cannot manage this tonnage and it would all end up pooled in a lake somewhere, becoming stagnant so that the fishy stench of rain is joined by the odour of rot and all the traces of decay.

Nonetheless, the fear remains, yet I'd be curious to pop your contact lenses, to gouge out your eyes, to stab your eardrum with the sharpest awl, to pour scalding hot beeswax down your throat, though there's no manual for any of this.

\*

It's not until late the next morning that you come back. At some point in the night, the teeming rain let up a bit, though it didn't stop. Looks like we can't go to the beach today, you say. You tell me the waves grew so violent in the night that they shut all the roads to the beach, which is when I notice you aren't even wet. There are lots of ways you might have kept out of the rain, so I don't ask any questions. You could have gone anywhere. I picture you sitting down, maybe holding or eating something, even vomiting it up. You could have been thrown down or rammed into, beaten up or battered. But the truth is like a blacked-out strip of film, a torn-out page, a pre-mixed dough—

You and I don't talk about what happened last night. We don't talk about whatever it is that clearly happened to your feet, about the things you've made real from all the infinite possibilities, and the still-unverified alibis and hypotheses we could choose to adopt or deny. You're worrying about where we can go instead of the beach, as if there was some way to rescue the holiday. Although this summer vacation is not a complete failure quite yet – there's still a lot left we can ruin.

In lieu of breakfast, we decide to go for a walk. Though it's too late in the morning to call it a morning stroll. In silence, as ever, we head down the steep staircase. There are spots where it's easy to lose your footing and, with gravity leaning, I know that if I missed a step and fell, you'd go tumbling, too. Every step makes me anxious. I'm not sure whether to fall or not. Your head wavers, nervous, making it too obvious for me to fall down the stairs now. The umbrella you left in the doorway is still wet. When you open it, one of the ribs is bent. I open mine. It's dry and taut like new, though it will soon be soaked.

A walk can take you anywhere so, as usual, we walk aimlessly. I don't think about all the places I want to go but places I want to avoid. In a similar way, I've made a list of people I'm not supposed to see, a list of foods I shouldn't have, things I'm not supposed to be doing, a list of the feelings I don't want.

I've no idea why we're walking in the rain, the wind splattering it onto our legs. Damp flyers flail around and stick to our shins. You peel them off to read. When we turn to go back down the street, the runners come past, raindrops on their arms as they strain to see, though it's not yet heavy enough to bother us and in fact falls a bit too gently for my liking as you toss another flyer to the wind. It gets picked up and swept away and I feel a sudden, deep anxiety. But this anxiety is only one part of the role I have been assigned.

Our walking is machine-like, fulfilling set directives with a certain method – a regular speed and direction – to produce a number of foreseeable results and some incidental ones. Rounding the corner is your role, and following behind you is mine, hiding my anxiety from you so that you don't notice anything is wrong, you notice but don't let on that you notice – our roles turning like cogwheels, until we come across the sunflowers again, and find they have been uprooted.

Should we go back? Let's go back.

Without saying anything else, we go back along the road we came up. You spot a pet shop which we didn't see here yesterday. Leaving me standing under my umbrella, you go into the shop and come out holding a plastic bag. We return home.

The yellowed bathtub is so small that only one person can squeeze inside it. Water streams down. From the sky to the earth, from the tap to the bath. The plastic bag with the fish inside floats in the bathwater, a tropical fish, though we aren't in a tropical region. You keep going in to test the temperature of the water. I figure if we release the fish into the bath water it'll probably die, but I don't fully trust my opinions. The image of a dead fish, belly up, comes to mind, along with the smell of disinfectant although it all feels like a dream I've had before. You keep popping into the bathroom to check on the fish. Now and then, you talk to it, your voice a low hum that I don't want to hear.

You poke your head out of the bathroom and say that we'll need something to feed the fish soon. What should we give it? I don't know the first thing about fish aside from the fact that they eat fish food. I've hundreds of thoughts firing in my head, though none of them offer any information on what fish eat. You head towards the front door.

I'm going back to the pet shop to ask them.

Uh-huh, got it.

The front door opens and shuts. The tap is on, the water still running, I'm staring at the bathroom ceiling, the fish swimming around inside that plastic bag. It must be raining still. Where was that swimming pool we wanted to go to? I try to think as I lie on the floor, but I can't picture one. The blue tiles on the pool walls, the cold water, the drain glinting silver – I can't place any of it.

They're becoming a problem, these things I can't speak about, or even name, or can only describe through a process of elimination. Things without definite shapes, with murky reasons. I should think about more concrete things, imagine only things I can feel on my skin, all the sentences in this tiny room churning out the same words over and over—

Nothing is concrete because the scales won't tare, because nothing can be placed on them when they won't stop shaking. I've nothing to hold onto. With all the dead cells cascading off me and the strands of my hair littering the floor, scales are impossible to rely on anyway, and it might seem as though I would absolutely *love* that but, honestly, the truth is, I don't.

Until you get back, I'm not going anywhere. I won't
go after you, won't even leave this room. It's impossible.
It's not possible for me to even want to.

*

You're not here.

You're not coming.

Our mini-vacation is over.

The windowless room is as pitch black as ever. The
only light comes from the bathroom. I wonder whether
it's the overhead light that makes the bath look so
yellow, though the bulb overhead is a regular fluorescent
one; I look at the water filling the bathtub, the light
green colour reflecting off its surface, and the fish you
released and left there. The fish stops, gently swaying in
the bath before darting forward, wriggling back to life.
I watch it for a while. When the water rises above the
level of the tap, the surface goes still, the bath running
without a sound. The torn plastic bag lies discarded on
the bathroom floor.

I only ever try on feelings, slipping them over my
skin, though they never seem to stick – it terrifies me,
pretending to feel more than I do, and I wonder if perhaps
I've never experienced any emotions of my own. I think
about refraction – both refracting and being refracted

– and I feel now the dull, hazy sense I get the day after I've had a lot to drink, my eyes intently following your retreating back.

Some seats go unoccupied forever. There's so much you can do with losing lottery tickets and reserved tickets for untravelled destinations and dug-up flowerbeds and lies. In the same way blood vessels betray the blood, cells betray the muscles, the spirit betrays the body, or the other way around, the way the pen betrays paper or the characters betray the book, I will continue to say ill-advised things: I'll kill you, curse you, wish you'd just disappear, may your days be filled with never-ending misfortune; unleashing all the words I've heard somewhere or other, words I've stuck together so badly you can see the glue around them—

I've lowered my hands into the bath. The water has risen and spilled, displaced, over the sides, soaking my knees, puddling already under my feet, the bathroom floor not sloped enough for the water to do anything else. I've spread my fingers as wide as I can, studied the muscles that strain in the backs of my hands, bent my wrists back and forth, yet the fish has continued to slip from my grasp.

I can't keep hold of its wet, wobbly body. Its razor-sharp scales leave tiny scratches on my palms. Some cuts are so deep that blood flows from them, though it's hard to identify the strange sensation with hands so wet I can't control them. And despite the vague fishy smell, when I finally manage to grab it and hold onto it with all the strength I have, I feel the fish is both firmer and more frail than I thought, so none of what follows happens as I'd imagined. Its gills really start going, its mouth opening and shutting, and I wonder how long I can wait like this. I give up on the idea of catching the fish. The cuts sting and I'm getting sleepy. I leave the bathroom with my soaked knees and damp shins and hands still dripping water.

*

You can torture someone even in the smallest room, even use the room's small size for a particularly effective torture. I am unrivalled at torturing myself, able to get into the source of my anger in painstaking detail; why I am ignoring it; why I am destroying it repeatedly. Although I don't want to do that now. Claustrophobia, my predilection for fear, the sheer terror that compels me to run away even though I always end up coming back, the joy of self-deprivation – I am forever trapped under these stories, which bear down on me differently each time I tell them, though it's fun to dream of being crushed to death.

I want to go in the pool. But I don't want the cold water and the sensation of my brain freezing up, and I don't want to immerse myself and get my scalp wet and then have to get out. I don't want the feeling of not being able to breathe, of hands around my throat, fingers and fingernails digging into it, then the blackness of the dark, the chill of the cold. No, I just want the cold water, cold enough to raise goosebumps on my skin, to rouse each of the villi in my body as the water runs down my throat, to somehow stop my heart and all the peripheral nerves and capillaries and all the dead skin cells that haven't yet detached.

There are moments when you have to choose one path or the other. Although these moments always make me pause. I don't want to give anyone the grounds to judge me, though this never stops them. For the sake of my story I would happily erase you. I don't want to add anything that might be seen as 'plausible'. No, instead, I'll have you open your mouth, close your mouth, speak or breathe or swallow or spit. I can clearly see your tongue wriggling around, and I swear I don't imagine one of your blood vessels wrapped around that crimson organ, have no urge to damage or cut or sever it. I'm always cruellest when faced with absence, and when I am alone in the room without you, I focus hard on the expression you would

108

pull, an expression that although I can't see it, it feels as though I can, as if this might be something I could give you, or maybe something you prepared for me.

(I'm not able to wield the sharpest tragedies, these meaningless and senseless speculations, which will have to here remain unfinished—)

# Loaf Cake

Sand was so angry he couldn't stand it. It would have been better if angry were all he was but he was angry and sad and lonely and miserable. Even worse, Sand was Sand and couldn't be anyone else, so not only could he not know what measures other people took when they were angry and sad and lonely and miserable, but even if he did it wouldn't have helped him in his particular situation. Far worse still was the fact that Sand had no idea what was making him so glum.

Maybe it was because his feet were always so clammy.

Or because he never got enough sleep.

Or because his flowers were always withered.

Or because his bread was always stale.

Or maybe it was because there was nothing wrong at all.

Sand cursed his clammy feet and insomnia, his withered flowers and stale bread with all his heart, yet nothing changed. Sick and tired of finding no answers in all this suffering, Sand made up his mind to leave home.

I tried everything to talk him out of it. Look, I told him, you always say you're in a bad mood, but that's all it is. Come on, I'll buy you a new bath mat. Then you can wipe your feet nice and dry, and maybe you'll feel better. Or what about some loaf cake from that bakery that just opened up around here? If you store loaf cake right, it'll keep for ages. And it's chock-full of nuts and dried fruit, so you can be sure it's tasty. And it might not be a bad idea to pick up a few flower pots on the way back from the bakery. Once you have a nice spongy mat, a whole sugary cake, and beautiful new flowers, you're bound to get a good night's sleep.

But no matter what I said, Sand only shook his head.

Thanks for saying all that, he said, really. But no matter what you do, nothing will change. A new bath mat won't make me less angry, and a tasty loaf cake won't make me less sad. All the flower pots in the world won't make me less lonely, and even if I manage to sleep for hours and hours on end, I'll still be miserable. There's nothing anyone can do about it. That's why I have to leave.

He dragged out the laundry basket from under the bed. Then he took out the suitcase from the closet and started stuffing it with books and notebooks, pens and toiletries, his laptop and earphones. You would never know from the perfectly serene look on his face that he was so angry and sad and lonely and miserable.

I asked, Do you really have to leave?

He didn't answer.

How about you think it over for a week – no, a day?

But he only continued to pack. I studied the neat stacks he made of his things. He closed his suitcase and pressed down hard on the top to zip it shut. Don't go, I wanted to say, but Sand – determined not to leave so much as a speck of himself – rose to his feet, hoisted up his suitcase, and said goodbye. Then he disappeared right out the door.

He had left traces of himself everywhere in the room. Looking around where his things used to be made me realise I had only ever been a visitor here. I lay on the bed that had once been his, in this room that had once felt familiar and dear but now seemed strange, no longer his at all. Soon enough, sleep took me.

The next morning when I woke up, I couldn't speak. Truly. I opened my mouth and moved my tongue and jaw in an effort to say something, but all that came out was my hot breath. I tried mumbling in a small voice, whispering in an even smaller voice, shouting in a terribly loud voice, then belting out a song that Sand and I both loved. But not a single sound came out. I could no longer speak, mumble, whisper, shout, or sing.

It made me angry. This was all Sand's fault! Yet I was also sad; in the end, there had been nothing I could do for Sand – angry and sad and lonely and miserable as he was. Now that he was gone, I was lonely, and now that I couldn't speak, I was miserable. Sitting on his bed, angry and sad and lonely and miserable myself, I got to thinking. About how I hated Sand, and how I worried for him. About how I wanted him to hurry back – though without any idea where in the world he'd gone, I'd no way of knowing when he might return.

I decided I would wait for him in his room.

Every day I tidied up that Sand-less room of his. I had no idea where to find his cleaning products, which made me think he'd taken even those with him. Eventually, I had no choice but to take the underground back to my house, gather up all the cleaning supplies I owned, and bring them back to his. I dusted and mopped and polished his abandoned furniture until it shone. I cleaned in silence, busy wiping down things that didn't need to be wiped, and dusting off things I had already dusted. No matter how much I wiped and wiped at the dust, it never seemed to go away, and no matter how much I scrubbed and scrubbed the furniture, it always seemed to be stained. As the room got darker I couldn't tell whether the dirt was really there or not. And, by the time I stopped, half the day had gone by.

Being unable to speak wasn't so bad. Perhaps I was well suited for silence. The only person I ever spoke to was Sand anyway. Finished with the cleaning, I sat down in his chair and leafed through a book of his. I nibbled on a bit of the bread he had complained about, and waited for him or any word of him.

But Sand's room was too small, its store of books and bread too little. He'd never kept many things here, and had taken so many books with him that there were barely any left for me to read. I read them and re-read them and then read them again. Tired of going back to the same books over and over, I longed to go on a trip to the library or bookshop, but I would have felt awful if he were to come back while I was out, so I had no choice but to return again to those same books I'd already read. In the end though, Sand did not come back, and just as the dirt from my fingers was starting to turn the book pages black, I made up my mind to visit the library.

*

The shop with the loaf cake I'd wanted for Sand was on the way back from the library. I'd only ever eyed the cakes in the window, never once going inside. I thought about all the things I'd promised Sand, how he'd rejected them, and where he might be now. I pushed open the heavy glass door. Maybe today will be the day he comes home, I thought. Little bells chimed above my head as I entered.

The bakery was in fact a shop with a few sets of tables and chairs inside in standard cafe decor. The furniture was gorgeous, white and gleaming. Behind the sleek black counter was a huge silver coffee machine. Framed by a big glass jar of coffee beans, little espresso cups, an assortment of mugs in all different colours, shapes, and patterns, and some tall drinking glasses, two employees were sat, talking behind the counter – one chubby and squat, the other tall and long-limbed. The tall one was waving his hands around, in the midst of a fascinating story.

The loaf cake was sitting there in the display window. Dried fruits were sprinkled on its smooth brown surface, and over the top of these shone a sugar syrup glaze that had hardened as it cooled. I could see nuts embedded within layers of a perfectly-cut slice. That colour is exactly what you'd call *golden brown*, I thought, as the tall employee with the long face approached me. His name was etched in white on his black plastic name tag: Snow.

Shall I cut a piece for you? he asked. I wavered, uncertain.

Sure enough though, the loaf cake I'd wanted for Sand was delicious. It was moist, with just the right amount of nuts inside, giving each bite an interesting texture, both soft and crunchy. The dried fruit was also on the inside, sweet and tangy and chewy. With every forkful, the syrup cracked like glass. In the blink of an eye I found I had eaten the entire thing.

A few days later, I stopped by Snow's shop again. Sand still hadn't come back. I felt sad and lonely he still hadn't returned, though also pleased that I could stock up on things for him while he was away. If I liked something, Sand was bound to like it, too. I pushed open the glass door and stepped inside the blinding white of the shop. The loaf cake was there, in the same spot as ever. I should buy a whole cake this time, I figured, not just a slice. I opened my mouth to call one of the employees, though no sound came out. And they were especially busy today as well. Unsure what else I could do, I stood dumbly in front of the display for so long that the sweat that had beaded up on my forehead began to cool.

Ah, said Snow, noticing me eventually and coming over. You're the one who came by yesterday. Do you want to buy a cake? Go on, take your pick. The bakery might be small, but we make all sorts of things. Everything you see is baked in-house.

He seemed very chipper when he spoke. I realised there were, in fact, several pastries next to the loaf cake, but I didn't want anything else. I pointed to the cake.

You must really like this cake, Snow said as he took it out. Do you live far from here?

Sand's house was in a different neighbourhood, and I couldn't guess what sort of distance Snow meant by 'far', so I said nothing. He seemed to take this as affirmation. He turned his back to me and started looking around for something.

It's really hot today so the syrup might melt, he said. I'll give you some ice packs to take with you. When you get home, you'll want to refrigerate the cake right away.

I nodded my head once, very hard. Snow slid the loaf cake he had painstakingly boxed up into a plastic bag, then fitted in the ice packs on either side. Relieved he had nothing else to say to me, I held out my credit card to pay.

It was at that moment, just as I was scribbling my signature on the pad, that it happened.

I meant to ask – can you not speak?

He made a series of complicated gestures as he said this. I didn't answer.

Don't you know sign language, then?

The cash register made a noise as it printed the receipt. Snow took out a pen from the pencil holder on the counter. I turned the receipt over and answered each question on the back: *I don't know how. I could never learn.*

If you want, Snow said carefully, reading what I'd written, I could teach you.

I shook my head. It wasn't as if I was desperate to have a conversation, so why bother? And there was nothing I really wanted or needed to say. My ability to speak had left along with Sand, so surely everything would be okay once he returned. I held the bag with the loaf cake in one hand, grabbed the crumpled-up receipt with the other and left the shop. There would still be ages to go until the end of the day.

*

Slowly, I grew accustomed to the topography of the world outside Sand's room. Although it was still hard for me to leave the house and head down to the main street without him, once out, I could get to the library, the supermarket, the convenience store, the swimming pool, and Snow's shop. I wished Sand was there to see me and how well I knew my way around.

One day at the supermarket, I ran into Snow. I was there buying a bath mat for Sand's room. But right next to the bath mats was a display of house slippers, and beside that was another rack in the middle of the aisle stacked high with baby powder. I had a hard time deciding which Sand needed most – even after I'd promised him a new bath mat, he'd still left. To make matters worse, the bath mats on the shelf were all light pink. I went back and forth between them for a while – soft pink bath mats, big cotton slippers the colour of matcha, white baby powder in kilo tubs. In the end, unable to choose, I began putting one of each in my trolley.

That was when Snow appeared behind me. Oh – you're the one who came to the shop that time, right? he said.

In my surprise, I dropped the bath mat into my trolley. I hadn't expected anyone might speak to me. Snow put one of the same pink bath mats into his own trolley. You must live around here, he said, smiling. You should come by the bakery more often. The hand that wasn't gripping his shopping trolley was busy waving around in the air. I offered no particular response.

Well, I'll see you around, said Snow, pushing his trolley on. I watched him leave, and as soon as he was out of sight, I took the bath mat out of my cart and set it back on the shelf.

I saw him again at the checkout queue. He was talking the ears off someone standing behind him. I went to stand in a queue as far away from him as possible. Over the heads between us, I kept seeing his hands fly up and disappear. Eventually, my queue moved until I could see the person with Snow. She was smiling and nodding her head.

Ma'am, please put your items on the conveyor belt.

At some point I had reached the front of the queue. Through the glass doors I could see Snow pushing his trolley towards the car park. Once I paid for my things and stepped aside, I spotted the person Snow had been with, putting her items back in her shopping basket. I saw now that she and Snow hadn't been together, but had been pushing their own separate trolleys all along.

He was always like that, I realised. Friendly and warm to everyone he met. After running into him at the supermarket, I went by the bakery every so often to eat loaf cake. Not because he'd invited me, but because I'd get hungry while reading and when I went to look in the fridge, I'd always see Sand's loaf cake there. I would eat away at it steadily, piece by piece, until I saw there was none left for Sand. Which was when I went to the bakery for another. Every time the glass door swung open, Snow was the first to react to the tinkling bell, rushing over to each customer to pour his heart into every little explanation, helping someone struggling to choose between this pastry or that confection, or doling out samples for people to taste. For those taking things to go, Snow stuffed so many ice packs in their bags that I wondered whether the pastries would freeze, for those eating at the tables, he always asked how they were doing and recommending them drinks that went best with their baked goods. If someone he knew passed by while he was out on the terrace, he could never just let them go, he had to greet them, and it was the least he could do to trim a crust off a castella to send them off with. Of course there were customers who found his overattentiveness bothersome, and others who came in the shop in a sullen mood, but Snow's smile never wavered, and the customers eventually calmed down and ended up laughing along with him, *ha ha ho ho*, carrying home bags of pastries in both hands. And when he wasn't doing all that, he was baking pastries, manning the register and grinding the coffee beans. His tiny co-worker seemed sort of relieved that Snow shouldered all this alone. Everyone grew to accept Snow's friendliness with a smile. No one found it off putting or uncomfortable. That was the part I found strange.

Every time I went to the bakery, Snow smiled at me and recommended different things. But I always ordered the loaf cake: one slice and one whole cake. I sat down at a table and waited for my piece, watching all the people coming in and out of the shop. Yesterday, Snow said, I put dried apricot in the cake, and today I used dried figs. I've tried all sorts of things, and I've found cranberries, figs, and almonds the most popular. But I still want to test out a few others. I might do peaches next as they're back in season. Oh, by the way, do you happen to have a favourite fruit?

No matter what he put in it, the loaf cake was always delicious. I would finish eating the slice he had served me on a little white plate, take the boxed cake and ice packs from him and then head home. On the walk back, I always swore this time I wouldn't touch the cake, that I would store it well, but sure enough, within just a few days it had disappeared down my gullet once again.

*

There was a big dog tied up to the terrace. It had a long snout and short, shaggy white fur and came up to about my waist. When I tried to make eye contact, it just avoided my gaze. The bell chimed when Snow stepped out of the shop and dipped his head in greeting.

He's mine, said Snow, getting down on one knee to pet the dog. He may look fierce, but he's really not at all.

I stood there, hugging a bag full of library books to my chest. I looked past Snow and through the glass door but didn't see anyone inside the bakery.

Oh, right – the shop's closed today, he said. I should've let you know before. Sit here for a bit before you go? You came all this way – I can't just send you back. I had been planning to take a break today, but I had some things to do, so I came by. Also, I had to practise my baking.

Behind Snow fluttered a paper that read *CLOSED TODAY*.

Come on in, he said. I'll give you a taste of what I baked today.

It was the same warmth he would have shown anyone, not only me. I wondered if there were times when he wasn't friendly, whether he had moments like Sand when he was so angry and sad and lonely and miserable that he couldn't stand it.

Snow switched on the lights, illuminating half of the shop. He pulled down two of the chairs that had been up on the tables. Wait here for a second, he said. He sat me down, then went behind the counter and grabbed all sorts of things – scones, muffins, madeleines, financiers, dacquoises, macarons, castellas, Baumkuchens – and set them out on the table. Every last one looked delicious. I didn't know which to reach for first, so I cast my eyes over them instead. Ah, said Snow, you'll need something to drink. Wait just a minute. He strode over to the coffee machine and returned with two mugs. A single ballpoint pen was tucked into his shirt pocket.

The dog's name is Crocodile. Because of his long snout, Snow explained. See? Isn't it kind of long for a dog's? Before I met him, I'd never seen a dog with such a long muzzle before. Lots of people think it's funny, having a dog named Crocodile. But I didn't mean it as a joke.

He told me that he found Crocodile abandoned near his former workplace, that he'd lured the dog home with some sausage, how long he'd taken to train and all the mishaps that had occurred in the process. I think of him as my little brother, said Snow.

Inwardly, I doubted the dog was as unique as he made out, as he went on and on, his hands moving relentlessly.

He realised I was staring at them – his hands, their constant motion.

Sorry, he said with a sigh. I know it's distracting. Old habit. Can't help it. Whenever I talk, my hands move around on their own.

He took a bite of a scone and frowned. Oh, this tastes awful – I must have messed up the recipe or something, he said, although I knew he was being modest.

Snow told me he had a younger sibling who couldn't speak. It hadn't occurred to anyone at first that the kid would never be able to talk. Snow said it was his fault, that he talked so fast and so much that his little sibling never got the chance to – which was what the grown-ups believed, too. So he learned sign language. Now he felt like he couldn't talk if his hands weren't moving. I hadn't asked him about any of this and didn't particularly want to know. I cut a castella into tiny pieces. There was no music on and the silence lingered. Suddenly Snow asked me a question.

Ah, right. We still don't know each other's names. What's yours?

I didn't answer.

Did it happen all of a sudden – losing your voice?

I didn't answer him then, either.

Isn't it a hassle?

I plucked out a paper napkin. Snow immediately handed me a pen. *One day, everything will be okay.* My handwriting was ugly but that didn't bother me. I hesitated for a moment, then added another line underneath: *when Sand comes back.* Snow's face creased slightly, frowning.

Sand? But the summer's already over, he said.

He could not have known about Sand. I considered telling Snow about him and how he'd left, but I just set the pen down. There was no use in explaining. Only one person in the world understood what it was like to live with Sand, and that was me. No one else knew the feeling of not being able to talk about the long wait for his return.

Snow and I shared some sweets. The dog was napping out on the terrace. After finishing two cups of coffee and the sweets, I left. Only a couple weeks before, the sun would still have been out now. I took my time walking back, drinking in the evening air, and when I came to the side street near the house, I realised I'd left the library books behind.

That Sunday, Snow and Snow's dog and I went to hang out at the riverside park. Snow brought some pastries he had baked.

This time I made bagels, he said.

He chatted with me, swinging a plastic bag at his side. He'd brought treats for Crocodile, chilled coffee in glass bottles, peaches and apricots he'd cooked down until they were soft, and a little plastic jar of tomato jam. He'd also packed a mat and a worn tennis ball that Crocodile liked.

We laid out the mat on the riverbank and sat down to have lunch. Snow spread the tomato jam on his bagel and took a bite. He told me he and the short, chubby worker at the bakery had made the jam together. We tried the peaches and apricots, too. With all the juice that dripped from them they were hard to eat. After a peach I had to go to the park bathroom to wash my hands. When I came back, Snow was feeding Crocodile a treat.

I grabbed the tennis ball and tossed it to Crocodile. He dashed towards it, caught it in his teeth, and brought it back to me over and over again. Soon, I got bored of playing with him. For a while, Crocodile amused himself by nosing the tennis ball around until at last he spotted another family with a dog and went to play with them. Watching the dog run off, Snow looked pleased. I liked how the bridge of his nose looked then, tanned from the sun.

After dinner, we decided to go to a movie. Snow tied up Crocodile outside the bakery.

Just wait here for a little while, he said. I'll come back and get you once the movie's over. You'll be a good boy, won't you, Crocodile?

He stroked the dog, petting his shaggy, white fur. Once we'd said our goodbyes, we got in Snow's car and headed to the movie theatre in town.

The evening news was on the radio. There had been an oil field explosion near the coast. Lots of people were reported to have died. I wanted to turn the radio off. I wished Snow would confess his love to me. The most whole-hearted confession of love in the world, which I'd dismiss with a withering look of apathy. That would be something to tell Sand when he came back: I waited for you the whole time. Anyone who approached me I drove away.

But Snow didn't say anything. I handed him my card. He bought the movie tickets, popcorn, and a coke, handing them to me one by one.

Just as we were coming out of the movie theatre, Snow gave me a potted asparagus plant he'd bought. I didn't even have the chance to turn it down or give it back. He explained how to care for asparagus. He kept moving his hands around even as he was driving, which made me anxious, but the flower pot was so heavy that I wasn't able to gesture or signal that to him, afraid the plant would fall over if I let it go. Even asparagus plants have flowers, Snow said. That's how you know they're growing well. They're tiny little flowers, so cute. At last, we pulled up in front of the bakery.

We heard no sound from Crocodile. Snow got out of the car first. I unlocked the door on my side but then I heard Snow's voice. Don't get out, he said.

But I was clutching the flower pot firmly with one hand and already pushing open the car door with the other.

I told you not to get out, Snow kept saying.

I went around the car and saw him kneeling in front of Crocodile. The car's white headlights were shining on Crocodile's cracked skull, limp front paws and fur soaked with something wet and dark. Whoever had done this, they had clearly focused their attack on Crocodile's head. In the dark beyond the glow of the headlights, someone had dropped a thick club. It bore a stain.

I screamed, but of course, no sound came out. Snow quietly lifted his hand. I saw the large shadow it cast over Crocodile's body and watched his long fingers start to rub at Crocodile's fur, soaked and caked with blood. He petted Crocodile like that for a long time. I was relieved that at least I didn't drop the flower pot.

Snow put Crocodile in his black car and drove away. I held the flower pot and started walking. I trudged home, the flower pot growing heavier as I went, until, just as I rounded the last corner, I set it down and stopped for a quick rest. My hips, hands, and shoulders hurt so I left it there and went home.

The next morning, the flower pot had vanished.

I didn't go to Snow's bakery for a long time.

And not long after that, Sand returned.

*

Sand came back empty-handed, the very same evening I learned that Snow had gone away. The short, chubby worker at the bakery told me the news. I was on my way back from the library, as usual. The short worker said Snow had quit a few days ago, after Crocodile's murder. You would never imagine something like that could happen, she said. To such a sweet dog, too. The customers won't ever get to see him again. Such a big, white dog. And his snout was so long. I swear, I never once heard him bark, let alone growl. It's just so horrible to think such a good dog could be beaten to death. Everyone in the neighbourhood knew he really loved that dog, and yet someone would still do something like that. I swear, there's nothing in this world scarier than people.

She was getting worked up as she spoke. We won't be able to make any cakes for the time being. You should look for a new bakery – I'm not sure how long it will take. It's hard to find people these days, she said, sighing deeply. With things how they are, I don't think I'll be able to keep the shop open at the moment. I'm really sorry.

I bowed a little. Then, hugging the books to my chest, I went back home.

When I got back, Sand was there. Sand, now as short as the pencil I'd been using the day before, sat on the sofa. Our eyes met, and I wanted to greet him. I opened my mouth really, really wide and tried to say the words: Hey. You. Came. Back. In. One. Piece. But all that came out was hot air. I stood in the doorway, mouthing dumbly, and started to bawl.

Startled, Sand asked, What's the matter? What's wrong?

I shook my head. Shook my head as tears shot down my face. Nothing, it's nothing, I said. But I wasn't making any sort of sound.

Sand told me he'd gone to the mudflats. At first, I was just walking in any direction, he said. I had no idea where to go, so I just kept walking, blindly trudging ahead, angry and miserable and lonely and sad. As I went on, I felt my body getting heavier. I thought it was because of my suitcase, right? So I opened it up and began to think about what I should leave behind. I thought I should get rid of the heaviest thing in there, but I just couldn't do it. Think about it – the laptop is expensive. And I saw I had way too much stuff in there anyway. So I was sitting there, luggage spread out all over the road, thinking I couldn't get rid of my clothes and how much I'd hate to have to leave the books, when this car came out of nowhere and screeched to a stop. *This* close to hitting me. The people in the car were furious and started swearing at me, and I shouted right back at them.

They took me to the mudflats. We sped along the motorway straight through the night until the mudflats appeared. And then, early that morning, I walked the road that ran alongside the flats, careful not to step foot on the mud itself. The flats were pitch black. I won't lie – I was scared. As I walked, my feet kept getting dirtier and dirtier. When I'd calmed down, I realised I had strayed from the road and was walking on the mud. My feet kept getting sucked in, and I couldn't pull them out. Trudging on and on was too hard and I soon ran out of energy. So I just lay down on my back, right there in that spot, said Sand. His hands were no longer trembling as he spoke.

He said he lay out on the mudflat, watching crabs no bigger than fingernails scurry in and out. I caught some of them and crushed them in my fist, he told me. I squished them to a pulp, which covered my hand in weird gunk, but I didn't want to wipe it clean. Then I just – I rolled around in the mud, screaming. I kept getting sucked in, deeper and deeper into the mud. It was such a weird, wonderful feeling! Before I got completely sucked in, though, these fishermen came and rescued me. If I'd rolled around there any longer I might've died, he said. Swallowed up by the mud.

I started walking again, going on for a long way. I even tried to go back and find the mudflats, but I couldn't. I'd come too far by then, and besides, I didn't know where exactly the mudflats were. The longer I walked, the heavier my suitcase became. So I just tossed it, right over the railings. It felt amazing! Afterwards, though, the sense of heaviness didn't feel any better. Weirdly enough, my entire body still felt heavy. It might have been because of the mud. Still, there was nothing for me to do but walk, so I walked. I thought everything in the world would resolve itself if I kept walking. However – increasingly in fact – I felt like something was off. Things kept getting bigger and bigger. Still, I just kept walking. I walked and walked until I was home.

And now I want breakfast, he said. Really bad.

Even as he'd been talking, he'd been shrinking, getting smaller and smaller in size. I got up right away and went to open the fridge.

We should cook up some bacon and toast some bagels, poach a couple of eggs, roast some asparagus and aubergine, then crush a few tomatoes into a juice and mix that with a peach puree to pour in some yoghurt to eat, he said.

As small as he was now, I thought Sand might be able to grow again if he had a really big breakfast. I took out the bacon and eggs, the tomato and the asparagus, and set them on the cutting board. Then I heard it. The sound of something going poof behind me. I turned around. Sand was gone. There on the shiniest possible hardwood floors, which I had worked so hard to clean, sat nothing but a little mound of dust.

## Ruined Winter Holiday

*Dear Sooyoung,*

> *How are you?*

I write the first sentence, then pause. Of course, I imagine she's probably fine, as I haven't heard any news from her one way or the other. Although now that I've decided to sit down and write her this letter, I'm drawing a blank on opening lines other than *How are you?*

I haven't written a letter in years, so I'm keen to open with something cool, the sort of line you'd hear in a movie, but as I never learned how to start a letter any other way than *How are you?* I end up just starting off the dorky way I was taught.

*Dear Sooyoung,*

> *How are you?*

It was on my way home that I got the sudden urge to write a letter. I stopped to buy stationery, although then it took me a while to think of someone to write to. Scrolling through all my contacts and friends, I couldn't help feeling the people behind all these familiar names were strangers and weird to imagine them reading a letter from me. I considered giving up on it all, though I won't put that in the letter. It would probably hurt Sooyoung's feelings. She would read the words over and over, brooding over them until she upset herself, every stroke of every consonant and vowel barb digging into her flesh. Just like the time she bought that broken music box.

It happened on our trip to Otaru. It was snowing that day, and our tour guide, who must have been in her early forties, brought us to a shopping district near the canal. I'd heard the music boxes there were famous, but thought, a music box is a music box – what could be so special about these? I went inside the shop to look around and saw you, hunched over on the other side of a desk, examining one of them. Everywhere in the shop, people were winding up and playing boxes, and the songs that poured out were all so similar I couldn't tell them apart. You stood up slowly, your eyes wandering towards me. There was a moment when our gazes almost met but, right then, someone dropped a music box.

It was Sooyoung.

Her box hit the ground with a loud crash. All you and I could do was stare and listen as a confusing flurry of foreign words swirled around us. I was curious to see all the bits and pieces of the music box scattered on the floor, but it had fallen somewhere out of my sight. It looked like Sooyoung had been going up the narrow aisle between glass display cases when her bag knocked one of the boxes and sent it plummeting to the floor. In the end, she bought the one she'd dropped, and was dealt another blow when she found out how expensive it was. Sooyoung was furious with herself for the rest of the trip and even afterwards, having wasted her money on an overpriced, unusable piece of junk. No matter how many times we told her not to be so hard on herself, Sooyoung remained inconsolable.

Of course, the real reason she hit the music box was because you had brushed by her just then and bumped her from behind. I couldn't tell whether you had done it on purpose, and it felt churlish to point a finger so I never brought it up with you. I just watched silently as you consoled Sooyoung afterwards. I didn't know what to say.

I'd like to put all this down in the letter, but I won't. She wouldn't want to talk about the music box. *Dear Sooyoung, how are you?* I still have no idea what else to write.

Why do people even write letters? In movies, the arrival of a letter would make a person remember someone or grow to hate them or forgive them or immediately fall in love with them – and even then they might come to hate each other all over again, killing or getting killed before the end of the film. But all of that only happens in movies, where the senders and receivers of these letters are clearly charming, despite their flaws, very loving and very easy to love. I'm a hundred percent positive I am not that kind of person.

I pick up the pen again and read back what I wrote. *Dear Sooyoung, how are you?* I hate my handwriting. By any metric it's pretty unappealing. I hear people have bad handwriting because they rush. It's impossible to write as fast as you think, and when you're trying to match the speed of your pen to your thoughts, your penmanship naturally suffers. But even while I struggle to think of something to say to Sooyoung, my words lose their balance and start listing as if they're about to fall over. I want to rip up the letter but if I tear it up just for how it looks, I'll never be able to write anything. I think fleetingly of all the scraps of paper already in the bin.

I don't know where Sooyoung is, so I can't discuss the weather. Here it's cold and dry, a layer of dust occasionally covering an otherwise clear sky. No matter how often I move house, the weather hardly changes.

*How is it with you? What's your life like there? Are you able to cope? Are you okay?*

I only have questions, though none she needs to answer: so much is already obvious. Of course there'll be people who hurt her and make her life hard, and days she slips up or does something wrong. As hard as life is here, I can take a wild guess and venture that it's probably just as tough wherever she is. Although she'll not be able to answer *How are you?* with anything other than *Fine*. Which leaves me, as always, just repeating the same meaningless sentences.

\*

It was you who said we should go to Hokkaido. The plane tickets are so cheap – we'll probably never see a deal this good again. I didn't really know what there was to see there, but I liked the sound of the place: Hokkaido. It would be a hassle to go that far though, and with me so hesitant to shell out the money, I put off giving an answer for as long as I could.

You joined a community of people sharing tips about travel in Japan, and almost every day you sent me hotel reviews or blogs about tourist attractions. If we booked the canal tour with a group, you said, it'd be a little cheaper. We might be able to find some travel buddies online. I didn't reply as I was amazed to see you so excited. For as long as I'd known you, you'd been mostly glum and listless.

In the end, I went on the trip because I wanted to see more of that side of you. It wasn't *our* trip but yours – I was merely a component, like the wheels or the handle of the 14-inch suitcase you rolled around. Everything was new to me, but I didn't hate it. In fact, I found it fun and had such a good time I sometimes wondered if the trip could last a little longer.

It occurs to me that it wouldn't be a bad idea to put this in the letter. If we can get onto anything aside from *How are you?* it should really be the story of how we all first met. *The trip wasn't my idea. I don't know if I've mentioned this before, but I'm not really the travelling type. Just the thought of going places I don't know, seeing new landscapes, carrying on conversations with people I've just met exhausts me. I like being in familiar places, with familiar people, enjoying the same old food I know so well, and coming and going without any fear of danger.* I think of sentences like these but can't bring myself to put them into writing.

The first time I met Sooyoung was the evening before the canal tour. We said we'd meet at the restaurant near where we were staying. She said she was also travelling with someone, so all four of us could sign up for the tour. Yet when we met, Sooyoung came alone. She said her friend had fallen sick suddenly and couldn't make the trip. I didn't fully believe her story, though soon forgot about it in my excitement to see the sights.

I learned that Sooyoung and I lived in the same neighbourhood, and that she had gone to the same middle school as you. I couldn't remember running into her ever though, and of course you couldn't remember what she'd been like in your middle school days.

How weird.

So weird.

Isn't it just the weirdest thing?

We went on like this all evening long. I didn't know what was so weird about any of it, but every time the word 'weird' came up again, we would giggle and order another round of beers. It got to the point we couldn't even tell what we were drinking anymore, but even that was pleasant. What I mean is, it was nice to be there – being one of a little group of three.

*

*Do you remember? We'd meet up every now and then after that trip. I might have mentioned this before, but I'm really not the travelling type.* I finish this sentence, add a full stop, then hesitate. A part of me wants

Sooyoung *not* to remember everything that happened between us. The whole reason I got to know her in the first place was because you said we'd save money by joining a group on the trip to Otaru, and even though I was reluctant to hang out with her without you, I still went along when she reached out. Honestly, there wasn't a lot to talk about when we met up. We didn't have that much in common. Meeting in Otaru, going to the music box shop together. Leaving it in a sulk, dinner at the restaurant that our tour guide recommended, agreeing on a time to meet the next morning, going to the airport in the same van.

The view outside the van windows was so unvaryingly white it bored me to tears. I was surprised how little there was to see at New Chitose Airport, nothing to do but nibble the triangular kimbaps we bought at a convenience store there. Mine had salmon roe in it, and with every bite the eggs burst and stained the white rice red. Other than being a little salty, it didn't taste of anything much.

I'm tired, Sooyoung said between intermittent bites of hers. I want to go home.

I could hear her choking up, on the verge of tears. Reaching to pick up her drink, she shifted forward in her chair, which jostled the broken music box inside her bag with a despairing sound.

I never want to go to Otaru again, Sooyoung said afterwards when we'd meet up. Just the name of the place makes me think of that broken music box.

I wondered what she'd done with the ruined one she'd had to buy, if maybe it was still in her bag, though I didn't dare ask. Whenever we talked about Otaru and the music box, Sooyoung looked physically pained.

Was it really that traumatic? I wanted to say, but I knew if I was too sharp, it would seem unfeeling of me. If I'm being honest, I'd always thought she made too much of it, but I kept my mouth shut whenever Otaru or the music box came up. She probably came to understand how I felt anyway. We spent more time sitting in silence than we did talking. Maybe it'd have been better if we had talked about you. But neither of us wanted to, and I don't know what we would have said about you anyway. It all meant that every subsequent time I saw Sooyoung, we said less and less.

You seemed to like her anyway. Sometimes, you told me what you two talked about. Which meant that when I was with you, I acted like she and I had never met up ourselves. I don't know why. Maybe it was because I didn't want to get close to her. When you two spoke, I worried that she'd bring up the times we had met. I didn't really think she would, but it bothered me to no end all the same. Weird, right?

I was your closest friend – yet it's hard for me to think of one thing I liked about you. Just as I had been to people, you had been good to me in some ways and awful in others, so much so that I couldn't say for sure whether you actually liked me or not. Sometimes it seemed like you had appointed yourself my closest friend in order to hate me, and other times it felt like you believed there was no one else in the world other than me you could talk to. So there were certain secrets I did everything I could to keep as secrets, although I never knew whether you did the same.

*

Where did we go that first day? I can remember getting off the plane late at night – maybe too late to go anywhere. The street addresses in Japan were hard to understand, and I recall you saying the iridescent blue signs outside Lawson's convenience stores were kind of scary. I said you only thought so because you read so many ghost stories – seriously, all day every day before the trip, you'd lie there scrolling through them nonstop.

I knew you'd be no use when you were like that, so the day before our flight, I threw together a list of famous tourist attractions, though we hardly used it. All the things you wanted to do sounded so intriguing

I let you drag me everywhere, like I hadn't done any of that research. Other than the aquarium (number one on your list) we saw pretty much everything you'd wanted; we wandered around all the sights, stopping only for snacks, and afterwards popped into the convenience store for beers on the way back to our place. Then we lay in bed and talked about all the places we had seen, and I listened as you told me ghost stories. You were always able to make a story even scarier than the original, and I was so terrified hearing them that I genuinely feared for our lives. Although, hearing your breathing so close beside me, my worries soon melted away.

When I heard you'd slit your wrists again, I rushed over in a cab to see you, thinking back to the sound of your breathing that night in that unfamiliar hotel room. I thought of the pattern on the ceiling looming over us in the dark like a fog, the blue convenience store signs you had thought so ominous, your voice when you told me you didn't think ghosts wanted to be bad, the cans of beer idle at our feet – a long, incoherent mess of memories. Things I didn't think about: the fun you had rolling an empty beer can with the tips of your toes, how happy you looked exchanging numbers with Sooyoung on the flight back home, your face as you told me about the great time you'd had on the trip, your feeling that now you'd be able to live your life to the fullest.

You said the wounds on your wrists weren't deep. I didn't even say hello, just looked down at you there in bed, eyes closed as if dead.

I'm sorry. Are you angry with me? I tried, you know. I really tried my best, but nothing worked.

It bothered me that your voice was so calm, so I didn't respond. I had also tried my best and also had things not work out, over and over, so many times that there was nothing I could say to you anymore; getting your own apartment came to mean you were able to seal all the gaps and leave the gas tap on; getting a car meant you could start it up one day at dawn, drive out of the car park, and smash right into the guardrail on the side of an empty road. It came to mean that you didn't have to be on edge all the time, didn't have to wait for that incessant voice in your head to completely disappear. If it never went away, you could jump or throw yourself off something. You could shatter a mug and use its pieces to sever your arteries, and take a pen from your pencil case and stab yourself in the back of the neck with it. It was you who taught me these things.

After I visited you in hospital, there were other times you tried to kill yourself. You had tried a few times in the years I'd known you, but then you'd seemed alright for a while, during which I didn't know how to handle your anxiety. I doubt I could do any better now, but the most I could do back then – as your closest friend, the person you were in touch with the most, as much your guardian as anyone who would never really be your guardian – was simply stay by your side.

I didn't often think about Sooyoung. Once, when I heard her name, I had to go through all the people I had ever known – granted not a long list – to try and remember her. That was how I found out she had moved somewhere far away, which was sudden, though not exactly a surprise.

It was you who told me she had moved. I guess everybody goes away someday. I remember your voice had been sort of rueful.

I nodded. Right. Oh, well – I suppose there's nothing to be done.

I couldn't muster much emotion, and oddly enough, when I tried to picture Sooyoung, I couldn't think of anything but the look on her face when the music box shattered. I used to think she looked so kind when she smiled, and I liked her slow, easy way of speaking, although these details seemed so foreign to me then, like the words you read on the back of the shampoo bottle as you wash your hair.

Nowadays though, I wonder if things would have been better if we'd just cut off all contact with each other. It would have been a chance to spare ourselves any of the news we didn't want to hear. I also wonder about all the other possibilities, though since the past is made up of all the futures we have or haven't chosen, it's probably meaningless to think about any of it. I didn't hear where Sooyoung ended up. And I heard about you less and less.

*

*Today was such a weird day. I mean, things have been weird for a few days since the family of stray cats I was feeding suddenly disappeared.* That day, a former co-worker got in touch out of the blue to tell me she was getting married and then, directly afterwards, my parents called. We talked for a long time without saying much – a wearying conversation. Two packages I was expecting were delivered to my old address by mistake, which wasn't a big deal, but I found it strangely exhausting. *I guess that's why I wanted to write,* I put in the letter, then pause. I don't want to seem like I'm justifying it and can't think of a reason that doesn't feel contrived.

I didn't want to be the sort of person who'd hurt you. Looking back, I may even have hoped you and Sooyoung would become closer. She was timid and passive, and riddled with anxiety, and even though liking someone doesn't always mean they'll be good to you, it seemed this was what you hoped. I think this was why I couldn't talk to Sooyoung about you.

If liking someone means hoping their situation would improve, then I certainly liked you. Although now I'll never know what you thought about it or if, indeed, it meant anything to you at all. I liked you because you mattered to me, so I decided that, more than not wanting to hurt you, I didn't want you to end up hating me. Maybe I just wanted to leave you to somebody else, not because I wanted to be your friend instead or even to help you better, but because, selfishly, I needed a place of my own I could be lonely in – these excuses are probably the absolute worst.

I feel like trying to defend myself any more would only make things more awkward. *I know why you had to go so far away.* But I don't write that. Instead, I write about how I've moved too, all the times I've changed jobs, then quit working altogether, how I packed up the house where I lived alone to move back in with my parents. I don't mention the music box, but I can't *not* think about it. Before I put the words to paper, I say them quietly to myself. The hum of the 'm', the fluid lift of the 'u' and the fall of the 'sic', then 'box' that ends it all with a decisive thunk.

Within the wooden box is a mainspring, which is connected to a small metal cylinder with tiny holes pierced all the way around it, which sits next to a comb with little metal teeth that pluck the holes as the spring unwinds and the cylinder slowly rotates. Depending how it breaks, the outside may not look any different. I wondered for a long time just how 'ruined' Sooyoung's music box truly was. The more I thought about it, the more disappointed I felt that I'd never actually seen it.

You could, I suppose, destroy things you had never touched. After all, it wasn't as though the music box had been damaged by her handling it – no, it was more like her failure to handle it was what had destroyed it, the way an untended plant dies from neglect. Even though she'd immediately stooped to gather up all the parts, there must have still been tiny pieces she wouldn't have been able to recover.

*Although, Sooyoung, I can't see how I can send this letter as you vanished without telling me where you were going.* And yet I know the truth all too well. If I had contacted her first, if I'd told her I heard she was moving, wished her well and brought up all those other nothingy words and phrases, she'd have gladly told me where she was going and for how long, and what she'd gone to do. I just know she would.

*I was really surprised you left so suddenly.*

154

A lie.

*I'm doing well.*

A huge lie.

I straighten up in my seat and look down at the two letters on the desk in front of me.

\*

I have this dream sometimes where I cut up people's names. Your name and those of other friends, coworkers and family members, people I've known only in passing – all the names I've learned and forgotten appearing on these lists, and I do my best to cut them out, mince them up, tear them to pieces that I crumble and mangle, then wipe, fretfully, off my hands. Every time I wake up from that dream, the hands on the clock are always in the same position.

I was no good at taking in my surroundings and soon found I'd killed several houseplants over the winter. I didn't know what exactly each plant had died of and had no interest in finding out. Maybe it was simply because that was the winter you died. I didn't go to the funeral. I knew it was cowardly of me, but I couldn't get my body to move. The cold air seemed to stun my muscles, my nerves. Which was my excuse. Though I hated not being there for you, I'm sorry that my body refused to cooperate.

*Sooyoung*, I write. *Did you go to the funeral?* But this sentence seems somehow stilted. Like something out of a language textbook, though I'd never learned *funeral* in any textbook I had seen. When did I even learn the word in Korean? No matter how hard I try, I can't think of when we'd first learned what *death* meant, or what *meaning* means, or why you kept slicing and torturing your skin with the same dull knife when the veins wouldn't sever.

I read your will again.

It was your older sister who told me about your will. I was shocked to hear you left me something. I had no intention of opening that envelope, yet there were signs that it had already been opened. I met your older sister for the first time after so many years. Although she looked so much like you, I immediately sensed her explosive temper. Maybe she was that irritable all the time, maybe it was because we were talking about you, I never found out.

Now, at my desk, I slowly copy out the sentences you wrote in it. My handwriting is still ugly. Afterwards, I add: *Sooyoung, what do you think?* Then I read back the line. My words really do look like I've copied them from somewhere. Like lyrics in a song I'd heard so many times it's become like background noise. Still, my heart is pounding, so I cover up what I've written with my hand and write *Sooyoung* underneath. The moment the music box fell to the ground, I had been looking at you. And yet, before that, Sooyoung was who I had been watching. I was thinking how pretty her eyelids looked as she bowed her head, her eyes half-occluded and wisps of hair falling over her pale forehead. I was studying her as though she could not see me when she suddenly looked over and I looked away. *Sooyoung*. I read her name again. It looks strange, this name I haven't said in a long time, although I've known it for so many years that it's still strangely familiar. Just like Sooyoung's face, staring at that music box. A look I know by heart, though I haven't thought about it in an age.

*

I have no happy memories, nothing like a souvenir I can take out and hold whenever I long for that chill winter air. And with no address, I'm left only with this letter I can never send, and the memory of a broken music box I can never hope to find.

# Shard

I wanted to sleep. Without nightmares or even auspicious dreams, without any sense of duty or guilt, as though sleep were my life's work, the only thing in the world I needed to do. But it was easier said than done and, once again, I found myself awake in the middle of the night.

Carefully, so as not to wake P, I climbed out of bed and went to the living room, where I found the dog asleep – front paws laid one over the other, ears slightly folded. A tiny lump, gently rising and falling. There was no easy way around the dog, so I gave up on going to the kitchen and squatted down in front of it. What a strange, curious creature; how on earth could it sleep so peacefully? Crouched like this, my shoulders and legs soon began to ache and I felt the dog's moist, warm breath on my toes, which quickly became unpleasant.

However, I remained crouched there for a long time, absentmindedly watching the dog before I got to my feet. The strange little creature stayed there, unmoved, like nothing I could do might wake it. The second hand ticked loudly as it made its way around the clock. It was dawn – I should have been sleeping. I dragged myself back to bed and tried to get to sleep again, but I just lay there the whole time, remaining awake.

\*

I wish I hadn't picked up that red ball. But there it was, sitting at my feet. A rubber ball a little smaller than my fist. I just scooped it up. It was soft and squishy – a bit flat. I rolled it around in my hands, wishing I had a pump. Although, just then, I noticed one on the ground next to me. I stuck the needle in and started pumping. The ball swelled up fast, became firm and round. It was nice. I rolled it in my hands again. It was smooth and rubbery like an eraser though with a frosted sheen. I bounced it off the floor and caught it. Then I threw it at the wall and it bounced right back.

I played mindlessly with the ball like that for a long time. The ball had a mind of its own. When it bounced off in unexpected directions, I ran as hard as I could to catch it. I was having such fun it took me a while to realise I was sweating.

As the ball traced a sleek arc in the air, it grew from the size of an apricot to the size of a peach. I liked the feel of it, its surface as soft as peach fuzz, held so closely that at first I didn't notice the ball getting bigger.

It grew and grew, faster and faster. One second, it was the size of a peach, the next a grapefruit, then somehow as big as a melon. I couldn't be sure if it was really getting bigger, or if it was just moving so fast I couldn't judge its size anymore. In my efforts to catch it, I jumped, slid, kicked, and swung my arms around like a wild woman, yet it only ever grazed my fingers before flying back towards the wall and then bouncing right at me again.

It really had me in its sights. It was now as big as an heirloom pumpkin and I had to run hard to avoid it. I figured that, with no wind blowing, it wouldn't change its course. Although I should have known better: the ball seemed to be mocking me, repeatedly bouncing off the wall and flying towards me.

It grew bigger still, ballooning to a size I could no longer compare to any fruit or vegetable and, as it swelled, it became more and more translucent. I could see into *and* through the ball, both the white wall behind it and my own terrified face in its reddish skin. Trying to escape, I tripped over my own feet and fell, unable to gain purchase on the surprisingly slick ground.

The ball was everywhere and nowhere, grown so large that it was completely transparent now. Every time it came bombarding through the air, I heard a whoosh then, as it hit the ground, a loud twang. I tried to figure out where it was, but with the sound reverberating everywhere, I couldn't tell which direction it was coming from.

And then, at some point, I was running again, my legs weak and failing. Don't step on your glasses, a voice called out, then twang, whoosh, dribble dribble, twang. That once-red, now transparent ball – which no longer seemed to be a ball at all – had to be flying at me from *somewhere*. My whole body was drenched in sweat. Can you sweat in your dreams? I wanted to stop running to check, but then twang, whoosh, dribble dribble, twang. The ball was at it again.

It's a rubber ball, a voice said. Why not hit it?

The idea was tempting. But because I'd never seen an *infinitely* growing rubber ball before, I hadn't yet realised it would never stop growing. It was big enough now to block out the sky and, forcing my reluctant legs to keep moving, all I hoped was that I might soon wake up from this dream.

*

That was the morning we were planning to pick up the dog. On waking and staring blankly at the wall, I had a feeling that the situation was somehow caused by me picking up that ball. Having to move all of a sudden, searching for a roommate, meeting P on a message board, finding out how well our personalities clicked – it seemed to all spring from that moment I picked up that red ball in my dream. I even imagined it had played a part in the decision to take in the dog. A ridiculous idea, I know: that present-me was somehow watching my future dreams give rise to past events.

I still wasn't confident we'd be able to look after a dog. There were my mild allergies and constantly-running nose, as well as all the various expenses, big and small, that pile up when you take on the responsibility of a pet. Neither P nor I had ever owned a dog before which made me worried about whatever unexpected accidents might occur – as well as any reluctance of ours to the changes a dog would force on our routines. Not to mention the leather sofa we had bought just a few weeks before. Myriad reasons not to do this kept coming to mind.

We had long, intimate talks about the dog, what our lives might look like if we had it, how we'd be changed by it. And, after a long time, it was decided: we were getting the dog. P's mind was made up, and I couldn't talk him out of it, no matter what objection I raised. Every time I opened my mouth, I shut it again. We *had* to bring the dog home – out of the goodness of our hearts, out of compassion towards a helpless living thing. I couldn't get my head around P's objectless affection.

But the decision was already made and I gave in. The whole matter was resolved last weekend.

All week, P was beside himself with excitement. He was constantly in touch with the dog's owner. I call her the 'owner' though she was just the person who'd found the poor thing wandering the neighbourhood. P showed me a photo. The dog was incredibly well-kept for having been abandoned: no scars, no fur falling out in clumps or anything like that. Its slightly up-turned nose, long sleek ears and utterly fearless face made it look even more like somebody's pet.

The woman said she already had several pets and couldn't afford to take in another. She put up flyers, posted on social media, and even asked friends and acquaintances, but no one got in touch to claim the dog.

P buried himself in research about how to look after a dog. But the more I thought about it, the more I felt my certainty slipping. I should have been firmer. But it's not easy to steel your heart like that. In the end, any willpower I had was squashed beneath the stack of delivery boxes that piled up in front of the door. Watching P gleefully open them, I felt as though my happiness and his – and the dog's, too – would forever be weighed against each other. This set of three-plated scales existed only in my mind – unable to rid myself of my anxiety and restlessness, all I could do was face the weekend looming towards us.

*

No one could say exactly what they were. They were simply 'the triangles'. Every week, one or two of them fell from the sky. Wherever they fell, they remained. At first, everyone thought they were going to destroy the city. But they had no weight and landed without any impact. Nor did they have any thickness. No volume. No mass. And yet just the sight of one – red or blue and twice the size of an adult man – sailing straight down from the sky and implanting itself in the ground was menacing. People instinctively retreated from them, watchful in case they walked into one or it fell directly on them.

From the top of a skyscraper, they looked like slivers of coloured glass studded throughout the city. At sunrise and sunset, you could see the light glint off the triangles' ultra-thin edges and radiate outwards, the multicoloured shards reflecting all the light around. Their beams pierced the fragments, splitting and fusing again, the triangles casting patterns onto the whole city. It was a dazzling sight. Like the entire city was surrounded by stained glass.

No one dared to approach them.

The triangles were all that anyone spoke about. Cult leaders proclaimed them heralds of the apocalypse, which was the easiest, least intellectual explanation. Looking up at the apex of one, its sharp gaze slicing downwards from somewhere out of sight, people ran their eyes along the sleek line of its hypotenuse and indeed saw a portent of the end of the world – the earth splintering into glass-like shards, the universe disintegrating into sharp, angular pieces. Although the world would not come apart in such a precise and aesthetic manner.

To me, they always seemed like props on a stage set, though that might have been because I was working as a stagehand at the time. I finished work at dawn most days and, coming out of the side street by the theatre, I would see a dark restaurant and a petrol station. Passing the corner shop and moving towards the main road, I'd see the edges of a triangle faintly glowing under the streetlights. A subtle citric glow spreading out in lines. Drooping flowers clung to the thick, wiry leaves that flashed in the light.

I imagined them cut from acrylic panels and suspended from wires. Although, of course, panels would have thickness and volume, weight and mass, as well as minute nicks and scratches; they would be nowhere near as crystalline as the triangle I came across on my early morning walks home. Our stage lights were strong enough to smooth away the nicks in those panels and I wondered whether aiming them at the triangle would create a similar bokeh effect.

My job at the theatre consisted of moving the light machines around, wrapping and unwrapping things in cellophane, installing wood flooring, dragging in fake walls and pushing them out again. I carried around cases of water, crushed plastic bottles, broke down cardboard boxes to stack them flat, took apart the houses built of timber and planks and cotton, their pulleys and wires, cogwheels and chains. At the end of every performance we were left with massive amounts of rubbish.

The work was fun, in its own way. After making the props, I could marvel at each one's ornate beauty and found a strange pleasure in the process of destroying them. We climbed the steep theatre staircases, arms overflowing with rubbish and props. What I loved most about the job was that I got to see the plays for free. As I worked, arranging the props in the wings, I could enjoy each performance up-close. It meant I never got to see the scenes as they were intended to be seen, but that was fine. From the table read to rehearsals and all the way up to the play the audiences saw, I could remember – and mirror – every line, every gesture, every one of the blocked routes the characters travelled across the stage.

*A lone hardwood table sits on the stage. On the table is a vase. A bouquet of cotton stalks. The actor's cold look grazes them. He doesn't touch them. Instead, he grips a rag doll's neck in his hands and pulls. The slight tear in it splits open, and cotton spills out. We see the ruined doll's face. The actor's hands gripping that face. Tense veins on the backs of those hands. Unrelenting pain. And 'scene'.*

A rubber prop knife, dropped and left on the floor, looking surprisingly real though it couldn't do any actual damage. The true hazard was the toxic atmosphere among the people who took apart the knives and other props. I didn't really fit in with the theatre people – mostly because I had gotten the job through a friend of the director's – and there were a number of tensions I didn't understand. Ones that couldn't be calmed by the greetings we exchanged or the meals we shared or our routine surface-level amiability. A vague sense of disaffection had settled over everyone, the result of an accumulation of small differences between us. A feeling – or a premonition – that things were getting worse.

The lighting operator and the director were the ones who shaped this atmosphere the most. The director was the type of person who always needed someone to pick on. Most of the crew members saw this and avoided needless conflicts with him. But the lighting operator was different. He had a retort, a counter, a quibble for everything the director said, now and then even poking holes in the director's ideas. Each time he did, the director became even more cruel, spewing words that would dismay anyone within earshot. I think the lighting operator wanted to prove himself by standing up to him.

Luckily, their feud didn't impact the quality of the plays. Although they often carried on like sworn enemies, they were still able to cooperate when they needed to. Which was the most unnerving part for me, as there wasn't much I could do in those situations; whenever the two of them raised their voices, all I could do was try to focus on the task at hand and pretend not to hear them.

It was on days like these that I'd stop and study the triangle on my walk home, wondering whether to approach it, whether to rush over and get to the bottom of this mysterious phenomenon. Or whether to leave it unexplained.

I decided to approach it, though I bound myself by certain guidelines. Curious to know if it had sides, I walked around the enormous wall of colour in front of me, peering at it closely. When I stopped in a certain spot, it was as if the triangle had disappeared. But one step to the side and the triangle loomed at an angle, glowing translucent yellow or sky blue. Then, when I stepped back again, vanishing completely.

People soon grew accustomed to living amongst the triangles. With no thickness, volume, weight, or mass, they seemed most likely harmless, and people quickly came to feel at ease around them, not paying them much attention anymore. They were simply *there*, fixed in place like movie theatre screens.

I thought it was wonderful having the triangles around, to see how they shone in a great kaleidoscope of colours when the sun beamed down on them. Fewer people worried about disaster, more and more out in their sunglasses. Going for a stroll between the luminous screens became a small, languorous delight.

*

The dog's guardian lived in a suburban town we had to take main roads and even the motorway to get to. As the one who'd insisted we go and pick up the dog, P said he would shoulder the burden of driving us there. It didn't make much difference to me. We got up early and loaded the car with all the pet supplies we had bought. P brought along the DSLR he hadn't touched in a long time.

I hope we can take lots of pictures, he said, setting the camera down on the backseat and shutting his door.

The engine revved into life. The sunshade was spread out over the window. I put the passenger seat back and saw my own gaze in the rearview mirror. I opened my eyes wide and stared hard.

The weather was nice, the sunlight warm. The traffic wasn't bad at all for the weekend, and we cruised along the motorway. I heard the soft hum of the engine, felt the faint vibrations in the car seat as we drove on. I wanted to sleep. Without nightmares or even auspicious dreams, without any sense of duty or guilt, as though sleep were my life's work, the only thing in the world I needed to do. P turned on the car radio to an afternoon programme. The host was reading a listener's letter in a low, gentle voice – a steady murmur. I turned to look out of the window. Vines crept up and along the noise barrier of the motorway. We went past rusty streetlamps. Cracked and peeling paint. A discarded styrofoam box now filled with small plants, their thin, tenacious roots, their little leaves. P concentrated on driving. Now and then, the young female voice of the car's navigation system informed us of the speed limit. My eyes slowly fluttered shut.

When I opened them again, P was getting back into the car. We were in the car park of a motorway service station. He offered me a takeaway coffee cup beaded with water droplets.

You were out for the count, he said. Rough night's sleep?

I took the coffee, nodding. P didn't know about my insomnia. The drink was cold, the cup filled with ice. I stirred the coffee around with the straw. I didn't like how the whipped cream had melted into it. I took a sip, then put it in the cup holder. Naturally, P couldn't help picking it up, wiping the condensation off it, then drying his hand on his pants. The beads of water on the inside of the domed lid bent the sunlight. P gripped the steering wheel again and I studied his neat, sturdy nails. The slight pink colour in his fingertips. The pale backs of his hands, stippled with hair. Soon, teeth marks would mar those smooth hands, leaving them forever disfigured.

*

P was one of the few people who had walked through a triangle. It'd been more of an accident, the whole thing happening because of a bet he'd lost when he was drinking with his friends. They were young and impetuous and looking for kicks, the more dangerous the better; if you were reluctant, all the more reason to do it. And so, drunk at dawn, no one else around other than his friends, P approached the triangle.

On many occasions afterwards, P would recall the incident, though all he remembered was his approaching the triangle and then the moment after having gone through it. In the stillness of that moment, P moved as he always did, with the same posture, the same gait.

There was nothing palpable that he could feel in the triangle. It had no smell, either. Reaching out to feel his way forward, he could only see its surface and then his fingers as they disappeared into it, as though he'd submerged them in a pool of black water. P pulled one arm back and reached out with his other, then took another step forward. All of his body slipped soundlessly through the red translucence the same way.

And in just five steps, the triangle was behind him. He heard a sigh. The red triangle, then its surface membrane – that was all he remembered. Just five steps and it was behind him. He felt neither dejection nor elation. What happened had simply happened: his passing through.

P recounted the story of him and the triangle, and I told him about the time I'd spent making and taking apart stage props in that underground theatre, watching all the scenes from the wings. That might have also been when I told him about those nights I'd spent alone creating a mobile. There were times I stayed until dawn, finishing up miscellaneous tasks before assembling it out of leftover cellophane and white string, triangular ornaments dangling from its rods. Naturally the director would have been furious had he known I was using the theatre's property for this, but cutting out the bits of cellophane was so much fun. The finished thing wasn't as beautiful as I'd hoped and, not even a day after finishing it, I ended up dumping it in the bin.

P couldn't remember how I'd looked when I was telling him the story. Which, of course, wasn't the only thing he couldn't remember.

\*

All of a sudden, I felt a little jolt and the sensation of my body falling forward, then my shoulders slamming back against the seat. The indicator on the dashboard was blinking. The light went click-clack, click-clack, click-clacked like a metronome.

I think we got rear-ended, P said, checking the rear-view mirror. You alright? It doesn't look that bad but I'll get out and check.

He pulled over onto the shoulder of the motorway and put on the handbrake. The owner of the car behind us looked like he was pulling over too. P took out his phone and started calling a number.

Actually, he said, would you mind going and looking?

I could hear the phone ringing against his ear. I tried to compose my face as I opened the door and got out.

Looking at our car, it seemed the one behind us had accidentally hit us when we were changing lanes. Which is what I explained to the other driver.

But when you change lanes, you're supposed to move over quickly, so wouldn't you say you've cut me off? the driver retorted.

I examined the car. Fortunately, the dents weren't large. Still in the driver's seat, P turned around to look at us.

The driver went on, As a matter of fact, since your friend there was the one who cut me off, should you really be here accusing me?

I looked back at P who'd opened his car door. I gave him a look that said not to get out. He was watching us with deep concern. The other driver looked me up and down.

Once the insurance person arrived, the issue was quickly resolved. I'd like to help, ma'am, if I can, he said. But we've seen more and more cases recently where the complainant was found liable for 100 percent of the damages. In a situation like this, it would be much better for you to settle. At least, that's my opinion.

He didn't look too confident though, sheepishly handing me a slip of paper with his details scrawled on it. I wrote out my own info in even more meticulous handwriting than usual. On the paper was a shadow. A strand of hair. I handed him the note and went back to the car. That was when I noticed the camera in the backseat had fallen to the floor. P picked it up and put it on the seat, then started the car again. The road was lined with hedges. My shoulders felt stiff. As we drove on, I thought I saw in the bushes the corpse of a mountain animal, now reduced to roadkill, but by the time I turned to look again, we had already come off that road.

P went on to live an exceedingly ordinary life. One that never required him to think about the triangles. He wasn't the only one. Before long, the triangles disappeared and over time, the summer we had spent watching them descend from the sky became nothing more than a vague memory. Whenever someone mentioned them afterwards, P talked about them the way he might have remembered seeing a celebrity on the street one day, or like an encounter with someone completely forgettable if there hadn't been photos of the pair of you, both smiling in strangely similar ways. That was all that remained of everyone's memories of the triangles.

Sometimes, P wondered about that moment he couldn't remember. Things like the exact angle of his right arm and index finger, the turn of his wrist, the image of the triangle shining in his retina, the colour in the iris formed by the building behind the triangle, like a transparent acrylic panel; the colour of the sign on the building, its letters, and all the dust motes floating beneath the light of the streetlamp that night he walked through the triangle. The only thing he could remember clearly was the red dust in the triangle's glow. In those moments, P wished someone had held his hand and walked with him towards the triangle. If they had, maybe he would have been able to remember it in more detail.

Sometimes I wonder if those guys didn't like me, P said one day. It was one of the doubts that nagged at him for years. I asked him why he'd think something like that, and he said there was no reason. It was just a feeling he had. I wished that he wouldn't think so much about things that had happened to him in the past. That he'd leave the unexplainable things unexplained. Not go near them or touch them again.

*

It was on the day of the last show. In the middle of the second act – a scene when five of the lights came on slowly at once – the light on the right side faltered a little and missed its cue. It was such a small detail it would have been easy not to notice. I had seen it from the wings, but nearly everyone was so busy attending to their own tasks they didn't seem to notice anything was wrong.

If the director hadn't become angry, they would have carried on unaware but while everyone was packing up the equipment, the director cornered the lighting operator and began to shout at him. He kept shouting the same things over and over again. To the soundtrack of wooden sets being broken down and paper tearing, we all heard him yelling, I could destroy every last one of you if I wanted!

It wasn't obvious if he was being serious, though he spoke with such vehemence it put everyone in the theatre on edge. I tried to focus on separating the cellophane sheets we used to wrap the lights but couldn't stop his words from burrowing into my brain.

Which was when the stage light fell. At the very height of their argument, the stage light fell and struck the lighting operator square on the back of his head before clattering on the floor. Chipped triangular shards rained out, iron crashing into wood. The lighting operator's body dropped to the ground. A scream rang out. The director gripped the back of the lighting operator's head, pressing down on his short hair as something slowly seeped between his fingers. Someone shouted, Ambulance, call an ambulance!

I stared at the ceiling, locked eyes with a stagehand looking down from the staircase that led up to the lighting operator's booth. His hand was trembling. I smelled blood. The lighting operator's head was swelling. A spray of red was gushing out. His veins were throbbing.

A&E was remarkably empty. A junior doctor was leaning up against the wall in the ward, nodding in and out of sleep. We approached the counter and a nurse who had been looking blankly at her monitor raised her eyebrows at us but said nothing. I heard a railway signal tolling faintly in the distance. Green floors. Brush strokes of paint hardened onto the walls.

A stage light fell and someone was hurt, I explained.

The nurse leafed slowly through some papers and pulled out several forms. Fill these out first, she said.

I watched the director trying to hold the pen as well as he could.

We stayed up all night outside the operating room. The toilet had faint green tiles and a rusted door handle that didn't lock all the way. Under the flickering fluorescent lights, a late-night baseball game was on in the waiting room. They showed replays of the baseball sailing over the fence. The hallway floors were studded with blackened pebbles of gum. I dozed off briefly and woke up about dawn. Slumped in his chair, the director said the lighting operator's family was taking an early morning train here. I watched the doctors move with slow footsteps, stethoscopes swinging against their chests. I decided to go for a walk, greeting all the nurses as I passed them, dark rings under their eyes. Outside, the sun was coming up. Triangles dotted the city.

I went towards the nearest one, a huge, dark-green triangle embedded in the ground. Just like all the others, it gleamed, translucent. I winced at its brightness but stood my ground. Widening my eyes made them sting and tears spill down but, undeterred, I refused to squint or shut them. I went around the triangle and saw for myself that it really did disappear at its sides. Then, standing in front of it again, I let out a deep sigh, wiped the tears from my eyes, and walked right up to it.

Peering through the triangle, I saw people like blades of grass or paper or rubber erasers. There were some who looked as brittle as thin plastic, and others round and gleaming like beads of glass. I walked forwards and moved through the triangle. The light was so glaring, it hurt.

\*

The owner was already waiting for us. The dog was playing beneath the table, a collar around its neck. It looked every bit the pet it had seemed in the photo, completely unafraid. The sun was starting to set. P took out his camera. Can you take a picture of me and the dog meeting for the first time? he asked.

I said I would.

When handling a dog, you have to first get down to its eye level and hold out the back of your hand. You need to give the dog time to get a sense of your scent. Once it seems comfortable, then you can slowly start to run your hand over its fur. P had read every single one of those pet care pamphlets aloud. He handled the first meeting well. I held the camera to my chest and pressed down so hard on the shutter that it took a whole series of photos in one burst, all of them very similar.

We brought the dog to the car. P started the engine. I sat in the passenger seat, just as I had on the drive over, and the dog rode in the back. I worried the dog would make a fuss while we were driving, but it was surprisingly calm and well-behaved back there. I looked through the pictures I had taken. The backlighting meant they hadn't come out well: P's hand, the dog's paw.

P was quiet, the only conversation coming from the radio. I saw the dog's black eyes in the rearview mirror. It hadn't moved once. Poor thing didn't seem to realise we were already far from its last home. It would probably never see its true owner again.

*

Damn. I should never have picked up that red ball.